GARRY KILWORTH
DRUMMER
BOY

Mammoth

First published in Great Britain in 1998 by Mammoth
an imprint of Egmont Children's Books Limited
239 Kensington High Street, London W8 6SA.

Copyright © 1998 Garry Kilworth

The right of Garry Kilworth to be identified as the author
of this work has been asserted by him in accordance with
the Copyright, Designs and Patents Act 1988

ISBN 0 7497 1019 5

10 9 8 7 6 5 4 3 2

A CIP catalogue record for this title is available from the British Library

Typeset by Avon Dataset Ltd, Bidford on Avon, Warwickshire
Printed in Great Britain by Cox & Wyman Ltd, Reading, Berkshire

Contents

'In the abandoned Battery [in the heart of the Inkerman battlefield, while fighting was still raging] Drummer Thomas Keep, a boy of ten, had made a fire to brew tea for wounded.'

'Heroes of the Crimea –
The Battles of Balaclava and Inkerman'
by Michael Barthorp, Blandford Press

1 Redcoats come to Rochford

'Hey, Charley Bates! Get away from them horses! You're disturbin' them, makin' them jittery.'

High summer. The sky was royal blue with streaks of white-cloud mares' tails swishing across it. It was market day in Rochford in the county of Essex. The cobbled square, with its pump and water trough plumb in the centre, was full of noisy livestock.

Charley paid no heed but continued to crawl into the corrals.

The air billowed with black flies of all kinds, from large thunder-clegs to the smaller house flies, attracted by the animals and the rotting vegetables. Pens held cows, pigs, sheep and horses, which stamped, bellowed, grunted and bleated into the cool morning air. Steam billowed from their mouths and rose from the soiled straw beneath their feet. Gypsies with red kerchiefs round their throats were trading horses with farmers in leggings. Both drove hard bargains.

'Did you hear me, Charley Bates? I'll have the law on you, I will.'

Around the stocks and pens people were milling, talking, shouting, yelling over the heads of others. Dogs ran in and around their legs. Chickens imprisoned in wicker cages clucked in alarm. Cockerels crowed. Men in frock coats and men in short jackets were noisily selling or buying animals and goods.

'So help me if you don't stop botherin' my ponies, Charley Bates, you'll feel my stick across your back.'

Charley Bates collected the horses' dung. He would mix it with straw and make manure to sell to gardeners for a few farthings.

Charley had long tousled hair covered with bits of hay and straw. There was usually a grin on his face, whether his belly was full or not, even in the coldest weather. His mother was dead and his father wandered the country finding odd bits of work. He battled with other urchins for the fly-ridden dung of shires and cobs. Charley and the rest of the local children looked rough. Both boys and girls wore a kind of loose smock over their underwear, often stained with brown juice. Their faces, too, were dirty. They were ragged creatures who slept mostly out of doors because their homes were hovels too small to house large families.

Charley slept in a stall much of the time, kept warm at nights by Sam, an old dray horse. He sometimes stole Sam's oats when particularly hungry. Sam never seemed to mind, though if his master had known about the theft, Charley might have been whipped or sent to prison.

Suddenly Charley looked up as he heard the sound of fife and drum. His eyes grew round and his heart beat faster with excitement as he watched in wonder. A company of soldiers were marching past the square, out of South Street, into North Street. The soldiers were wearing bright red uniforms with white cross straps. On their heads were tall hats known as Albert shakos. Over their shoulders they carried muzzle-loading rifles with long bayonets.

Charley felt a stirring in his stomach as he watched

3

the soldiers go by. It turned to one of delight when one of the men cocked his head slightly and winked at Charley. Soon Charley was running after the soldiers, like many of the children, and he stood by while they set up a stall outside the Ship Inn.

Lieutenant John Pickering, bored-looking and testy, dismounted from his horse. He set up a trestle-table and stool. Then he took out a large ledger from a leather bag, along with pen and ink. These he placed on the table with some small ceremony, as if the gravity of the situation required it. It aroused even more interest.

'Listen, lads!' cried Company-Sergeant Bilford, as the crowd gathered. 'I want you to think on this – your country is at war with Russia and we need hardy men. The pay's good and the food's fine . . .'

'That's not what I 'eard,' yelled a voice from the crowd.

There was laughter but the sergeant took no notice. He was well used to interruptions. Instead he tried the tactic of going for an individual so that the crowd's attention was split between his victim and himself. The people had gathered to be entertained. The sergeant knew how to provide it.

4

'You, sir,' he said, picking on a tall youth of about seventeen, 'you look like the sort of English oak we're looking for! Tough, strong, out all weathers and not afraid of a bit of wind and rain.'

'Ar,' said the boy, 'but rooted firmly in this here ground, sergeant.'

The crowd chuckled.

'And wooden between the ears,' added the sergeant.

The crowd roared and slapped their thighs.

'Come on, where are the brave young Essex yeomen I'm told will fight for queen and country? Who'll take Our Majesty Queen Victoria's shillin'? There's foreign travel thrown in. You should see our lads in Constantinople – now there's a city to behold. Golden domes, emerald spires, rivers sparkling like crystal. And the pay's good, I tell you.'

'I've been told that after stoppages you gets left with only tuppence a day.'

Instead of disputing this, the sergeant grinned and opened his arms wide before the crowd.

'Tuppence a day?' he cried. 'Why, that's a bloomin' fortune to a lad like you. How many glasses of ale can you drink in twenty-four hours, eh? For there's nothing else to buy with your money. We gives you a smart red uniform which'll have the girls giggling like mad – we feeds you good, right and proper – we gives you a bed to sleep on. You can live like a king on tuppence a day – provided there's nothin' else required to make you comfortable. Think on it!'

And so this kind of banter went on, while youths sidled up to soldiers and inspected their weapons.

Charley went up to a tall, lean soldier who told him his name was McSween.

'Can I see your gun, mister?' he asked.

McSween, three upper teeth missing in the front, grinned at Charley.

'O' course you can, son, but it's a rifle not a gun. A gun is a big cannon. How old are you, boy?'

'I don't know, sir. I'm older than Sissy Wilkens, but not so old as Harry Bell, sir.'

McSween laughed and nudged his companion, a thickset, rough-looking man with a heavy beard.

'Hear that, Wilson? I'm a sir already. Only been in this man's army two years and already I'm an orficer.'

'Officer, you ignorant man,' Wilson said, 'and

the day you gets promoted even as far as lance-corporal, I'll get a pair of wings.'

Charley took the rifle and found it was quite heavy. He wondered how you could carry such a thing around all day long and not get tired. He admired its beauty. He heard one of the other children being told it would hit a target at a mile away. The bullet, said McSween, was no longer round like a ball, but shaped like a cone.

'Do you want to join the army, son?' asked the recruiting sergeant of a boy not much older than Charley. 'I could find a place for you in the band.'

'What would I have to do? Shoot people?'

The sergeant laughed and put an arm round the boy's shoulders.

'Why, not for a time, young master. In the beginning you'd play a fife or drum. You'd get to carry one of these though,' and he showed the boy a short sword. 'It's called a marmaluke and the only soldiers allowed to carry it are drummers. So, will you go for a soldier?'

The young lad stared around him at the red uniforms of the men in their shiny black shakos. His eyes were bright with the excitement of the moment.

7

It was obvious to all, Charley included, that the boy was sorely tempted. He stared at the drum which the regiment's drummer had placed on the ground. It looked a marvellous instrument, with its cords and straps and taut drumskin, not to mention the sticks which the drummer had whirled and rat-a-tat-tatted on the drum's wooden edge.

The sergeant nodded to the drummer, who picked up the instrument and straightened his body, his expression turning very serious. With the drum at a jaunty angle, the drummer set himself, beginning with the tips of his drumsticks under his nose like a moustache. Then he began to play, the sharp staccato sound echoing along the street. At first the rhythm was medium paced, but it gradually grew. Faster and faster the sticks whirled, racing out a martial tattoo on the skin.

Every man, every boy within earshot, felt a jolt of military fervour go through his body at the sound of that drum, especially when the fife joined in. Their feet wanted to march, march, march along with the soldiers, all the way to Portsmouth, over 100 miles, even if their heads told them it was a foolish notion. So long as that drum played, they were England's to a man.

Abruptly, the drummer came to a halt.

'Well?' asked the sergeant of the boy in front of him. 'Will you go for a soldier?'

Everyone waited to hear his answer. It was obvious that a great struggle was taking place. Finally, he shook his head.

'Naw, me dad would flay me alive when I got back home again – I'm needed on the farm.'

'What a shame. There's still a need for a drummer, then. Any strong young boy can join, though it would be better he told his mother and father afore he spoke up. Any boy here willin' to do that?'

There was no answer. Charley watched the sergeant's chest heave as he sighed. Then Sergeant Bilford began his act again for the crowd. One or two youths drifted forward to the table where the still-bored lieutenant sat with the book, waiting for them to make their marks. In the end, the sergeant had three recruits in his clutches, one of them the witty youth who had answered him back.

Once it was all over, the soldiers went into the inn, followed by a good number of the crowd. Charley followed and found himself a corner to sit in, while the soldiers got noisily drunk and insulted the serving

9

girl. In wartime soldiers were cheered wherever they went and got away with all sorts of bad behaviour.

Lieutenant Pickering sat aloof from the men. He sipped port and stared disdainfully at the local girls drinking with the soldiers. There was a medical officer with the squad of men, but the lieutenant avoided his company too. Officers in the regiments did not regard doctors to be true soldiers, because they did not fight. Only when wounded and in pain did soldiers cry out for their attention.

Lieutenant Pickering was a very arrogant young man, who had, like most officers, bought his lieutenancy – but he was also eager to be at the war. He wished to cover himself with glory on the battlefield, so that he could go home to his family with pride. His father was a baronet living in Thaxted.

The medical officer had no liking for Lieutenant Pickering or for drinking with the men, and he sat down next to Charley. He asked the boy his name and Charley told him. The doctor nodded at the soldiers.

'They make a fine noise, don't they, lad? When you grow to their age, be sure to remember how foolish they look when they are in their cups.'

10

'Yes, sir,' he said, looking up. 'Are you a general, sir?'

The medical officer laughed. 'Lord no, I'm just a doctor. Dr Porter's the name.' He looked at his pocket watch and saw that the hour was late. 'Are you expected home, lad?'

Charley looked up nervously.

'I don't have what you'd call a home, sir. I sleep in a stable with a horse called Sam. My dad's looking for work up in the north of the county. He can't take me with him 'cause I can't walk as fast as he can.'

'No mother?' asked the doctor, raising his eyebrows.

'No, sir. I have some cousins who give me food sometimes, when they have some themselves.'

The doctor sighed. There were children like Charley in the cities and country towns, who were not exactly orphans, not exactly abandoned, but certainly disregarded. They lived on cabbage stalks and crusts of bread. If they were strong they survived the cold winters. If they were not they froze to death in some back alley or hedgerow.

The parish was supposed to take care of those in need, but children like Charley did not want to go

11

into the workhouse. They avoided the parish authorities and had to rely on their own cunning and the generosity of others. Often their relatives were as poor as themselves, with large families to feed and house. They could not cope with another mouth.

'You had better get to your stable bed, Charley,' said the doctor, 'before these men start their usual quarrels.'

'Will they fight each other?' asked Charley.

'I would say that is almost a certainty – and possibly the village youths too.'

'Goodnight, sir.'

'Goodnight, Charley.'

The boy then jumped to his feet and skipped out of the inn doorway, into the cool night.

2   Gone for a soldier

Charley walked back to the stalls where he slept. He shivered just once, more with the excitement of the day than because of the coolness of the evening. Something was beginning to stir in his heart. His life here in Rochford, while not terrible, held no real prospects in store for him. If he lived to reach his twenties – not by any means a definite thing – he would probably become a roving farm-worker like his father, moving between farms as the seasons and harvesting of the crops dictated. Today a different sort of life had presented itself to him. He had a choice.

Above him was a clear sky encrusted with stars. Around him the summer breezes sighed through the trees. Burnished light from window lamps revealed his path, but he knew it so well he had no need of guidance. In the air was the tangy scent of plants from Mr Matthews' herb garden, next to the stables.

Charley crept into Sam's stall. Being high summer, Sam was out in the paddock, enjoying the balmy night air. Charley reached into his smock for a piece of turnip, which he chewed while lying on a bundle of hay.

He thought about his father. It was not that Charley did not like his father, but he did not know him. He saw him briefly, about twice a year. Charley had heard his aunt say his father had no sense of family responsibility.

Then there were his aunts and uncles, and his cousins, for whom he did have some affection. But, like his father, his uncles were all farm-labourers, bringing in a meagre wage. They lived in tied cottages, owned by the farms they worked. Charley's father hated the tied cottage system, which put the tenants for ever in debt to the farm owners so he preferred to work wherever he could find a place. Rents were always more than the families could afford. In any case, farm-workers took most of their pay in vegetables and meat, rather than money.

Since families were large, some with over a dozen children, the two rooms of the cottage had to be used as bedrooms. During the day the downstairs room also served as scullery, kitchen, dining-room and living-room. There were dogs, cats and chickens running around, too. One extra body was resented as a further burden on the family's poor income, so Charley preferred to be in a spacious stable. Sam did not grumble at him simply for being there. He seemed to enjoy the company.

More than anything, Charley wanted to belong somewhere. He needed a family, someone to whom he was special. Charley had not known love for long, but he knew he wanted to feel useful and needed. There was a special place in his heart for the misty memories of his mother, but there was no other person to whom he was particularly attached. He was a free bird, looking for a nest.

In the morning the cockerels roused him from his sleep. Charley immediately rose and went to the water trough in the square for a drink. He splashed water on his face. He found a wrinkled potato and some cabbage leaves, which stemmed his gnawing hunger.

Then he ran barefoot to the inn, wondering if the soldiers were awake, and found Dr Porter eating breakfast outside.

'Good morning, Charley. Did you sleep well?'

'Where are the soldiers?' asked Charley.

'Still asleep, and will be for an hour yet. They will rise with sore heads and grumble and complain, but it's all their own fault. Would you like a piece of ham, Charley?'

Charley's eyes opened wide and he nodded dumbly. The doctor gave him a slice of meat, which he wolfed down without a by-your-leave or thank you. He wiped his mouth on the back of his dirty smock sleeve and burped in satisfaction.

'That was good, mister.'

'Doctor to you,' said the medical officer.

Charley stayed around the inn until the soldiers were up and had been fed and watered. Then they were on the road again, the lieutenant and the doctor on their horses. They headed west for the ferry across the Thames River, and over into Kent. Some of the children from Rochford followed the troops along the dusty road towards Woolwich, gradually dropping away and running back home, all except one – Charley.

At noon the soldiers rested outside a wayside inn, where the men gratefully sank to their knees on a grassy knoll. Charley remained with them. The horses were allowed to graze freely on the verge. The doctor was not in the habit of riding such long distances and he walked stiffly away from his mount.

Even the new infantry recruits were good walkers. They were used to going on foot to work in the fields. Often they would cover ten miles or more each way from their homes to the farms and back again. These new men, not yet in uniform, were being lectured by Company-Sergeant Bilford. He was telling them they would have to smarten up their ways, that they were louts and layabouts, and that they needed discipline. Already they looked as if they regretted joining the army. The sergeant took pity on one man and told him to cheer up, for he would probably be dead by Christmas.

It was too likely to happen to be taken as a joke.

Amongst the veteran soldiers Private McSween was cleaning his rifle. Charley decided to speak to him.

'Why,' cried McSween, 'it's the young lad I saw yesterday in that town – what was it called?'

'Rochford,' said Wilson.

'They all look alike to me,' replied McSween

cheerfully. 'These English towns with their English cattle. What's your name, boy?'

'Charley Bates. And I want to play the drum.'

'You followed us all this way, eh? Sergeant, there's a fine strong lad here by the name of Charley Bates and he wants to be a drummer boy. Will you have him, sergeant?'

Company-Sergeant Bilford came over and looked down at Charley, who sat quietly waiting for the verdict.

'He's a bit small, an't he? What's your age, boy?'

'Eleven,' said Charley quickly. 'Or twelve – I could be more, if you asked my dad.'

'Don't know your own age, eh? Where's your pa now?'

'Gone away.'

'Mother?'

'She died.'

'No other family? No one who'd miss you?'

Charley shook his head vigorously.

'Will *you* miss anyone?'

'I like working in the summer, potato picking, or pea picking. And you should see the rabbits run out of the corn when it's cut. We chase after them to catch them for supper. Then there's the cows to bring in from the meadow, and Tinker, the dog, to feed . . .'

'*People*,' said the sergeant patiently. 'Will you miss any people?'

'Some people a bit, I think, but not much.'

The sergeant shook his head. 'You're a tad small lad – you may have to help lift wounded men on the battlefield. Did you know that bandsmen did that? They help the doctors.'

'I could play a drum,' said Charley, not really listening. 'I know I could.'

McSween said, 'Ah, take the boy along, sergeant, you can see his ribs poking through his clothes. He's just a waif and stray, so he is. I'll look to him.'

The sergeant stared for a little longer and then he nodded.

'Well, you look after him until we get to the camp, Private McSween. Listen, lad, do as this soldier tells you. Don't lag behind, mind, for we've a deal of miles to go yet. Later you can make your mark in the lieutenant's book. Can you read and write?'

Charley shook his head. 'Do I have to?'

'No, lad, for McSween himself cannot put pen to paper unless it's to make a cross . . .'

'And most of the others here,' McSween reminded his sergeant. 'I'm not alone in having no schooling.'

Sitting there on that grassy slope, the dry summer air speckled with insects, the breezes rustling through ditchweeds, and the smell of shorn cornfields in the air, Charley felt content. For the first time in his life he felt as if he *belonged* somewhere. McSween and Wilson talked to him as if he were one of them. He was not just Charley Bates. He was part of a family, a family of men in red coats. He sensed that they would not let outsiders harm him without retaliation. He would never be lonely now.

They let him look at their rifles. Wilson showed him how to load the weapon. He took a cartridge from a leather pouch on his belt and bit it with his teeth. He let the bullet and gunpowder fall down the barrel. A smell like pepper came up, which made Charley's nose tickle. Then Wilson took out a ramrod and rammed the powder and bullet to the bottom of the barrel. Finally he took out a percussion cap and placed it on a nipple below the sharp firing hammer.

'Then you cocks the hammer,' said Wilson, showing him how to do it with his thumb. The hammer was quite stiff and Charley managed to pull it back with difficulty. 'Aim the weapon,' Wilson said, standing behind Charley and helping him hold the rifle against his shoulder. 'Level it at that old oak over there. Up with leaf sight. Keep it true.'

All the men in the company were now looking at Charley. Some of them were grinning. The sergeant shook his head and said something to the lieutenant.

'Now *squeeze* the trigger, boy – don't jerk it – aim the rifle at the middle of the tree . . .'

CRACK! The rifle went off and knocked Charley flying backwards off his feet. He lay on his back amongst the grasses feeling frightened and dazed. His ears were ringing with the sound. Around him the soldiers were laughing.

Private Wilson retrieved his rifle as Charley sat up and rubbed his sore shoulder. When Charley pulled back the top of his smock, there was a bruise the colour and shape of a large plum.

'That hurt,' he muttered, fighting back the tears.

The sergeant said, 'All right, that's enough. You'll be injuring the boy. Leave him be. You've had your fun.'

When Charley sat down by McSween and Wilson again, they praised him for his courage.

Wilson said, 'Not many boys o' your age have let rip with a Minié, Charley. You did well there – and I do believe you hit that old oak.'

'Did I?' asked Charley. 'What's a Minié?'

'Why, that's the name of this here rifle,' said McSween. 'It's spanking new, the Minié rifle. We used to carry what we called the old "Brown Bess", which was nothing more nor less than a musket – but the Minié, now that's a true rifle.'

'And I really hit that old oak?'

'Saw the bark fly myself,' Wilson confirmed. 'Went zinging off the trunk.' That was something to tell the children back in Rochford square. Soon he would have so many things to tell he would not be able to remember them all.

'All right, on your feet,' called the sergeant, as the lieutenant mounted his horse. 'Time to tramp the road to Woolwich. We must be at the ferry in an hour.'

A corporal said to Charley, 'You be off up the front, with the other three recruits.'

'Why do we have to march at the front?' asked Charley. 'We'd be better behind until we learn how to do it.'

'Why,' grinned the corporal, 'to keep a weather

eye on you, that's all – to stop you runnin' back to your mothers. It's easy to slip away from the back of a column, lad, but up front you have no chance of escape.'

'I don't want to escape,' protested Charley.

'Maybe, but then again, the day is early yet – and there are others who I think might be off at the drop of a hat.'

So Charley went up to the front of the column, which marched in threes. He was placed in the row behind the new recruits, in between McSween and Wilson, who grinned down at him and winked. At first he got his legs tangled up with others but, after he had been shouted at by Sergeant Bilford for the sixth time, he managed to keep in step, his bare feet patting the dust road to the same rhythm as the men's boots.

However, he still found it difficult to swing his arms in the opposite direction to his legs. They seemed to follow naturally behind the lower limbs, right arm trailing right leg, left arm chasing left leg. It was too hard to think of keeping in step with the others *and* making his arms do things they did not want to do. One new thing at a time, surely?

Charley's heart began to soar with the feeling of

adventure. He was in the army! Not just that, he was going away, overseas, to places he had never heard of before. And there was still the treat to come of being given a red uniform to wear, with all the little straps and buckles that went with it. And a wonderful shiny black Albert shako. And bright new boots. And, finally, the short sword with a crossed handle. And best of all, people *liked* him.

'What's the best regiment in the whole army, boy?' asked McSween as they marched along. 'Give me your answer, quick!'

'Is it the 44th Foot?' asked Charley.

'And who are the 44th Foot?' questioned Wilson.

'Why, the East Essex Regiment,' cried Charley, forgetting to whisper. 'That's us, isn't it?'

The sergeant bellowed, 'Quiet in the ranks. When there's talking to be done, why, I'll do it all, if you don't mind, Private Bates . . .'

Private Bates. Did that not sound noble? Charley's mother would have been proud. Her third child, and the only one still living, now had a title as grand as any duke. Her Majesty's Private Charley Bates. Why, when you said it like that, it almost made you want to bow.

When they reached Woolwich, Charley was ready to drop with weariness. There were other companies of the regiment waiting to board the ferry to cross over into Kent. They too had gathered recruits from towns and villages. These men in civilian clothes all had the same half-terrified, half-bewildered look that Charley could see on the faces of the recruits in his own company.

'Company, *halt*!' cried the sergeant.

Immediately, Charley and the three new recruits sat down on the ground to rub their feet, only to have Sergeant Bilford scream at them to remain at attention in the ranks.

'Stand *still*, stand to attention, you 'orrible oafs. Have I stood you at ease? Have I stood you easy? Have I dismissed you from the ranks? I don't think so. Look at my soldiers! Do as they do. Hold your position at attention until you are told otherwise, or you'll find yourself on the wheel.'

On the wheel. Charley didn't know what that meant and when they had finally been told to 'Stand easy' – stand in loose formation, but not sit down – he asked McSween.

'They ties you to the wheel of a gun, then flogs

25

you,' he said. 'It's a punishment for doin' wrong.'

Charley swallowed hard.

'Does it hurt much?' he asked.

'It fair makes your eyes water. I've only been on the wheel once – fifty lashes for spittin' in the direction of an orficer – not even for spittin' *at* him, for they said there was no difference, though I didn't hit him at all – and my eyes were fair smarting I can tell you. Don't worry, they won't flog you, boy, not till you've growed some.'

At last the order was given for them to break ranks and make a meal. McSween, Wilson and Charley found some driftwood on the banks of the Thames and boiled up a kettle, which McSween had been carrying hooked to his belt. They took salt beef and biscuits from their knapsacks. While they sat eating, Charley stared at all the men in uniform.

With the whole battalion now together, there must have been nearly a thousand men. He heard accents of all kinds: Irish, Scots, Welsh, West Country and North England. Some were difficult to understand, for though it was an Essex regiment with mostly Essex men, it recruited wherever it went.

A thousand men! There were red coats all around,

26

rifles stacked like sheaves of corn, hats scattered over the grasses, fires and kettles boiling in their tens. It seemed to Charley that no enemy could win against so many British soldiers. Surely this war they were going to would be over too soon, and they would be on their way back again?

3 A drum and a sword

Charley was on the third ferry to cross. The River Thames ran deep and brown and Charley stared down into its waters as if he could see his old life in there. His new life was on the other bank, waiting for him to start it. His new world rolled out in all directions, seemingly limitless.

On the other side of the river stood the waggons which would accompany the battalion to Portsmouth and beyond. They carried tents, food, blankets and other supplies. Charley was taken to Captain Shenke, the quartermaster, who issued him with a uniform which almost fitted.

The boots were much too large, but they were his

first ever footwear so Charley did not care. He was told to wear both pairs of his socks until his feet grew. Charley was immensely proud of his boots, thinking them the best present he had ever been given. There was also the bonus of some smart leather laces to keep them more firmly on his feet. McSween showed him how to loop these through the holes which ran up and down the leather flaps.

'You'll have to learn to tie a bow, lad,' said McSween, doing it for him. 'Don't go tying any tight knots you can't undo after a day's march, or you'll regret it.'

As for the beautiful scarlet coatee, all he had to do was roll up the sleeves three inches to find his hands, the same with the Oxford mixture trousers to find his feet. He was told that the regimental tailor would alter his uniform later, when he could get round to it, but Charley was already reluctant to let go of his uniform, in case it did not come back again.

'Is that a drum?' cried Charley, as an instrument was rolled out of the back of a waggon. 'Is that *my* drum?' He could hardly contain his excitement.

McSween told Wilson that he doubted if Charley had been more than ten miles from the centre of

29

Rochford before going for a soldier. His face was a picture as they crossed the Thames, and he wondered at the curving grey sail, the brown water, the taut sheets, stays and lines. Even though Sergeant Bilford bellowed at him every so often, for he was unaware of the many rules and regulations, Charley's pleasure could not be quelled.

Once the quartermaster had issued all the new recruits with uniforms, Dr Porter came to give them an inspection.

The examination was a cursory one, the doctor being more concerned with lice than looking at bodies. Nevertheless, Charley felt a flutter of panic in his breast. He edged away as the doctor walked down the line, looking into each recruit's mouth, asking them if they had any sores, enquiring about illnesses in the family.

'Charley,' said the doctor as the drummer boy tried to hide behind one of the big farm hands, 'are you afraid of me?'

'Yes, sir,' whispered Charley. 'It – it was my mum who went to see the doctor in hospital and never came home again.'

'Doctors are not here to hurt you, but to help you.

Now, I have to ask you some questions, Charley. Have you slept near any drains recently, or places where there is raw sewage?'

'Sir?'

'Open cesspools, that kind of thing.'

'No, sir,' said Charley, flinching when the doctor felt down his arms. 'Not that I know of, sir.'

'Stand still, boy. Just let me feel your limbs and tap your chest – it won't hurt. You're shaking like a leaf, laddie. Stand up straight, don't droop. Don't pull away, I'm not going to cut anything off. That's better . . . let's see your legs. No rickets? Good. No running sores? Eyes clear. All right, you can stop twitching now. I'm finished with you.'

Dr Porter went on to the next recruit, leaving Charley like a limp rag.

'Have you had any coughing or spitting of phlegm . . .'

Once Charley had been dismissed from the doctor's line, he was sent to the river to wash himself. He went in knee-deep, dressed in one of his new shirts, leaving his old clothes on the bank. While he bathed there came a yell from behind him. Charley looked over his shoulder to see a drummer boy holding up his dirty old smock. It was Private Daniel Swinburn, one of Charley's comrades-in-arms. He was nearly fourteen years of age and probably felt like a grown man beside Charley.

Swinburn brandished the smock like a ragged banner on the end of his short sword. He carried it to a campfire and threw it on. Under his filthy smock Charley had worn an old rough flannel shirt which had once belonged to his father. This too was consigned to the flames.

Charley ignored Swinburn and proceeded to splash himself gently, washing furtively under his shirt tails.

'Don't be too careful,' cried Swinburn, taking up a camp kettle and filling it. 'Be generous with it.'

Swinburn threw water over Charley, thoroughly soaking him, and handed him a bar of soap. Charley washed as best he knew how, but it was obvious that this was not a frequent exercise for him. Swinburn offered to scrub his back with a groom's horse brush for 'three farthin' ', but Charley glared at him so ferociously that the bigger boy did not attempt to make good his threat.

'You stay away from me,' cried Charley, 'or I'll get McSween to cut your throat.'

'Well, there's a nice thing,' grinned Swinburn, but without rancour. 'You've got some vicious manners, my lad. Never mind challenging me at fisticuffs, you'll get blackguards like McSween to cut my throat for me, eh?'

Charley did not reply to this, probably realising he had broken some code of conduct by hiding behind another man's shirt tails.

Swinburn felt there was something lacking in Charley. He did not seem to know the rules of manhood. It was not that he was a coward, for a craven boy would never have left Rochford. But it seemed he could not have cared less what others thought of his courage or willingness to fight his own battles. His pride ran in other directions. He was more concerned about how they felt about his company.

Swinburn confessed to McSween later that he had thought Charley a poor specimen of boyhood at first and considered scorning him as a friend. However, drummer boys really had to stay together, for they had no one but themselves in this world of men. Swinburn was forced into comradeship with Charley as the only other boy and Charley quickly came to worship the swaggering older boy. Few youths can resist being worshipped and Swinburn soon considered Charley his closest friend.

'I'll show you how to hook on the drum,' said Swinburn, helping a bewildered Charley into his straps and lanyards, once the boy was dressed. 'Here, look how your Albert shako rests on your ears – you'll have to grow your hair, my lad, to pad your headgear a little, eh?'

The little drummer boy looked as smart as any soldier in the camp. His drummer's uniform was laced round the collar, and up the sleeves and coat seams, with the regimental-pattern drummer's lace. Charley was immensely satisfied by this ornamentation and was continually fluffing it up and preening it. Swinburn showed him how to hold the sticks and then told him to beat his drum.

Charley made a racket which had all the soldiers within earshot yelling at him to throw his sticks in the river. Swinburn touched his nose with his finger, hooked on his own drum, and showed Charley how it was really done. Swinburn was a brilliant drummer and his sticks flashed in the afternoon sun as he played the regiment's favourite Retreat.

'Will I ever be able to play like that?' asked Charley breathlessly.

'Oh, of course,' said the generous Swinburn. 'I'll show you how – that's what I've been asked to do.'

Charley was deloused that evening. The fleas fell from him by the dozen. And his hair was cut short. Once he was clean he paraded around like a cockerel, wishing his mother could have been there to see him in his moment of glory.

On the following morning the march south began. The regiment had to go on foot down to Portsmouth. True to his word, Swinburn began to show Charley the rudiments of drumming, teaching him how to do a simple roll. Charley was not lacking in natural rhythm and learned his instrument fast.

In the meantime, McSween and Wilson continued to nurture their friendship with Charley. On the third evening of the march, they were camped outside the city of Winchester. The battalion had left the road at St Cross and had pitched tents at the bottom of St Catherine's Hill, under which flowed the River Itchen. McSween and Wilson called to Charley as he passed their fire.

'They are riff-raff, those two,' muttered Swinburn,

so the two soldiers could not hear him. 'You would be well advised not to have anything to do with them.'

'But they were kind to me when no one else was,' Charley said. 'I can't just turn my back.'

Swinburn went on to the bandsmen's tents, while Charley sat down in the place offered him by the two soldiers.

McSween said quietly, 'Will you be going into town this evening, Charley?'

'No, I think not,' he replied innocently, 'for Sergeant Bilford told me the city is out-of-bounds to us.'

Wilson nodded gloomily. 'Ah, yes – it's true – the place is off-limits to us soldiers. But for drummer boys, well there's a difference, you see. They often send drummer boys into town with errands. The doctor will want his medical supplies replenished, the officers' batmen will need boot polish, the canteen will need flour for bread . . .'

'Well, if I'm ordered in, then I'll go. I won't get into trouble if they send me, will I? Why do you ask?'

McSween looked over his shoulder into the darkness, carefully, as if suspecting he was being overheard.

36

' 'Tis a little matter of some cough syrup.'

'Cough syrup?' repeated Charley in surprise. 'Have you a bad cough, McSween?'

'Devilish bad one. It grips me in the night and tears me throat out. I need the consumptive mixture bad but, as you say, the town's out-of-bounds to us soldiers. If you go in, mind, you can get me a bottle of cough syrup by askin' at the inn – here's a shilling.'

'At the inn? What would they be doing with cough syrup? Are you sure you mean the inn, McSween?'

Wilson said sharply, 'If he says the inn, he means it, small fry.'

McSween rounded on his comrade. 'Softly – don't yell at the lad. Charley didn't know the Frenchies make this remarkable cough syrup, did you, Charley?'

Shadows flickered over McSween's lean face in the firelight, giving it the look of a hatchet.

'They do? What's it called?' asked Charley.

'Cognac,' replied McSween quickly, pronouncing it 'kognak'. 'Cognac. It's the French word for "cough". If you pass an inn, just nip inside quick and ask for cognac in a black bottle. They'll know what you mean.'

Charley took the shilling and put it in the pocket of his scarlet coatee.

'Certainly, McSween. I'll get your cough syrup for you if I have to go into the city at all. But maybe they won't send me on any errands . . .'

They did send him. They sent all the younger members of the band.

The sergeant warned them, 'Be sure *not* to buy any liquor for the men. There's an order out that they are not to drink on the march and even their rum ration is being withheld until Portsmouth. You buy what's on your lists and then come back here. No diversions into sweet shops, you hear?'

'Yes, sergeant,' said the young drummer boys, trumpeters and buglers. 'No diversions.'

They had to cross the St Cross water meadows to reach the road. Swinburn had a lamp and Charley stuck close by him, not enjoying the darkness of an unfamiliar landscape. Once out of the water meadows, the herd of boys crossed a bridge and went on into town, scattering to search for their various goods. Charley had only one thing to buy: a sackful of cheap candles.

'The candle-maker's is over there,' said Swinburn. 'You'll have to knock him up because he looks closed. I'll meet you in thirty minutes by the cathedral steps. Don't get lost, Charley.'

Charley was left standing in the cobbled street. A thin rain was coming down now, soaking his precious uniform. It was the first time he had been alone since he began following the soldiers. This was a foreign place. These were strange city streets, with their black cobblestones and iron-caged basements. A trickle of panic ran through Charley as he stood there, trying to make himself walk forward without the company of other soldiers.

Finally, he managed to get his new boots clumping over the cobbles. The sound of his own feet felt a little more comforting to him than the previous silence.

Soft yellow lights glowed in the houses and over the shops around him. A coach and horses came hurtling round a corner and went crashing by. Lit up on the inside, a hatted man's thin face peered out at Charley. For a moment he was petrified again, his breath caught in his throat. A few seconds later it was gone, rattling away in the distant streets, the coachman's gruff voice yelling at the horses. It had left Charley's heart fluttering like a trapped wild bird in his chest.

Charley calmed down and went to the candle-maker's door and hammered on it. Someone grumbled as bolts were drawn, then the door flew open.

'What?' said a grizzled, middle-aged man. 'I'm at my dinner.'

'S-s-sorry, sir,' stammered Charley, 'but I've been sent by the army to buy candles.'

'Have ye?' replied the man, straightening a little, 'and I suppose it's the cheap tallow candles ye want?'

'I'm afraid so, sir.'

He heaved a sigh. 'Well, business is business, even if it is with the damned army. I don't know what we want with ye. Ye come into our towns and make havoc, and then go off and have fun fighting the French, costing the country so much money . . .'

'Russians,' said Charley quickly.

'What?' the man exclaimed. 'What Russians?'

'Swinburn says we're not fighting the French any more, sir – we're fighting the Russians. The French are our friends.'

'As if it makes any difference,' grumbled the candle-maker. 'Here, how many tallows did ye say?'

Charley told him and the man fetched a sackful of candles from the back of his shop. He handed them to Charley, took the money and, without another word, shut the door in the boy's face. Charley slung the sack over his back and then looked about him for signs of a cathedral. He knew it was some kind of big church, but had no idea of its actual size.

There was an ale-house just down the street, so Charley decided to ask directions there. He went in and sought the serving girl. Girls were always more patient with him than grown men. Then he remembered McSween's cough syrup. The girl, harassed by yells from the patrons in every corner of the room, took the time to tell Charley the way to the cathedral.

'And I'd like some cough syrup, please,' Charley added with his thank yous.

'What?' asked the girl, running her fingers through her frizzy hair. She was not more than thirteen.

'Come on, you little hoyden, get me that ale.'

'A – a – a bottle of *kognak*,' said Charley, giving her the shilling. 'A *black* bottle.'

'Oh, you mean *cognac*,' she said, reaching into a rack behind the bar. 'That's brandy-wine.'

'No, not brandy-wine,' replied Charley, 'kognak.'

But the girl had already put the bottle in his hand and was halfway across the greasy floor with another customer's drink. It was a black bottle, just as

41

McSween had said. Charley put it into the sack with the candles, thinking he would mention it to Swinburn to make sure he had got it right.

Once outside he made his way through the night to the meeting place. The rain had stopped and the moon had come out, lighting the way for him. Charley found Swinburn waiting on the steps of the most enormous building he had ever seen. It reached clear up into the night, soaring stone that flew up and outwards. Or perhaps it merely seemed to go outwards? There were marvellous projections everywhere, and tall windows that glittered with colour in the moonlight. A monstrous doorway stood at the bottom of the steps, which had surely been made for giants to pass through. There were ugly gargoyles on the eves, still gushing rainwater from their mouths. They looked down on Charley with malice.

Above, a weathercock glinted on the corner of a tower. There were dark, tangled cloisters and mossy walls. Charley felt there were ghosts everywhere, waiting to pounce. He stood closer to Swinburn, who pushed him roughly aside.

'What are you doing? Trying to climb into my boots?'

42

'It's this place,' said Charley falteringly. 'Are there huge graves here, with great ogres in them? Why would they build it so tall otherwise? Look at that door, Danny. If you were three times as tall, you'd still pass through. This place, it's so big and spooky – I don't like it.'

'Then let's be on our way, you lily-livered loon. It's only a cathedral, you know. There are plenty of 'em. They build 'em so big in order to let God go inside – God's a big fellow, you know.'

His loud, clear voice echoed around the cathedral close, and through the cloisters.

'I don't think you should talk like that, Danny,' said Charley, shivering. 'The stone angels might hear you.'

Charley was staring at the carvings of creatures with wings and dull eyes, perched on gravestones. They seemed to be waiting for a signal to take flight. Danny looked also, and Charley saw a flicker of fright cross his friend's face. Finally, Danny spoke in a quickened, excited voice.

'You are a dope sometimes, Bates. Come on then, race you to the bridge. Just think of ghouls bursting out of the tombs, all dripping with rotten green flesh.

43

Think of white bone poking through their skulls and yellow teeth clacking in their great white jaws. You'll run twice as fast, my lad.'

And Danny was right, Charley flew like the wind.

4 Witness to a flogging

On the flight back to camp the two drummer boys overtook other young bandsmen. When they ran into camp the lights of many fires chased away their night terrors. They grinned at each other as they sucked in whistling breaths. Then they took their goods to the quartermaster. In the excitement of the hour Charley completely forgot about McSween's bottle.

They left Captain Shenke and made their way to their tent to sleep. Charley was pleased to be able to take off his boots. The leather was leaving blisters on his heels and toes. Still, they were warm, and once he got used to them he knew he would enjoy the feel and look of them on his small feet. He dropped into a deep sleep almost instantly.

An hour later both boys were shaken roughly and told to get outside the tent.

'Wha-what's the matter?' asked Swinburn.

Charley was too startled to say anything. He did not even have time to put on his coatee or boots. Shivering in the night air, he was marched to a large tent. Inside, Lieutenant-Colonel Peters was sitting behind a trestle-table. It was Charley's first sight of his commanding officer and he looked a fierce old man with white whiskers and white hair and weathered features.

Near to the colonel stood Captain Shenke. In the captain's hand was the black bottle of cognac Charley had bought.

'Well, sir, what have you got to say for yourself?' asked the colonel in a low but serious tone. 'Speak up.'

'S-s-sir?' asked Charley.

He was too stunned by the drama of it all to say anything. The colonel mistook his silence for guilt.

'What about you, sir?' asked the colonel, rounding on Swinburn. 'You were this boy's companion. Did you encourage the buying of the liquor? Who was it for? Answer now, or it'll be the worse for you.'

Swinburn was also astonished and dazed but, being older and more experienced, he quickly gathered himself together.

'I know nothing of the matter, sir. This is the first time I've seen the bottle.'

Once again, the colonel stared hard at Charley.

'What is *your* name? Speak up.'

'Bates, sir,' said Charley, his mind at last freeing itself from numbness. 'Swinburn is right, sir – he knew nothing of the bottle. It was me who bought it.'

'You bought brandy when there was a specific order out *not* to bring liquor into the camp,' thundered the quartermaster.

'Captain Shenke, if you please, sir,' the colonel said in a quieter voice. He stood up and glared down at Charley from a superior height. Speaking with slow gravity, he said, 'Now Private Bates, do you like brandy?'

'Me, sir? No, sir. I haven't ever had none.'

'Then why did you purchase it? Did you think to resell it at a profit? Was that your intention?'

'I don't know what you mean, sir. I just bought it

for . . .' Charley stopped, suddenly, looking out into the night miserably. 'Isn't it cough syrup, sir?'

There was stifled laughter from a group of officers and NCOs who were standing outside the tent.

'Cough syrup? Some might say it has medicinal value in certain circumstances, but only in small quantities. That is not *good* brandy, lad. It is rotgut, fit only for the belly of a man strong enough to take its harsh kick. I would say that is the tipple of a veteran soldier. No, it is not cough syrup.'

'I was told – I'm sorry, sir – I didn't know it was liquor – I was told to get kognak – shall I take it back to the ale-house?'

'Ah! You scamp!' cried the quartermaster, unable to contain himself again. 'You admit you bought it at an ale-house! Why would you think it cough syrup, you little scoundrel? Are ale-houses in the habit of prescribing medicines? Do they have doctors and chemists at their beck and call?'

The colonel again waved down the captain's choler.

'*Cognac*?' asked the colonel. 'Who asked you to buy cognac? Did the man who charged you to bring him this bottle tell you that cognac was cough syrup?'

'Y-y-yes, sir. Said it was French language for cough.'

'And what might be that man's name?'

Now, if Charley had learned one thing, it was that you did not tell on someone. Swinburn had told him that it was up to the army to find its own evidence against men it wished to punish. You did not split on a comrade, no matter what happened. You had to pretend you did not know who he was.

'I don't know, sir.'

At this point the colonel seemed to get as angry as the quartermaster had been. His white hair seemed to bristle as Charley watched.

'Tell me his name, boy, or you will be punished in his place.'

'I – I can't.'

Captain Shenke said, ' 'Twould be better if we cut the lad loose, here and now, colonel. Send him back where he came from. We have no use for brats who lie.'

Mrs Duberly, the paymaster's wife, a lady who travelled with the regiment, was just outside the tent. She was a young woman in a yellow dress which swelled about her in a buttery froth. Her thumbs and forefingers held up the hem, so that her petticoats did not trail in the mud. Her delicate pretty face below the dark hair had a complexion which Charley thought looked very much like the top layer off a jug of full-cream milk.

'Colonel, you cannot think of sending this child away now. He is miles away from his home. He will get lost and perish on the way.'

'I'm afraid, ma'am,' said the quartermaster, who thought that army business was nothing to do with army wives, 'he should have thought of that before disobeying an order.'

'But you heard the boy. He thought it was cough syrup.'

'Enough,' bellowed the colonel suddenly. 'It is I who must mete out punishment to the boy. He will go without rations for two days. If he still refuses to divulge the name of the man who corrupted him, I'll seriously have to think of sending him back to his home town.'

'But . . . ' began Mrs Duberly.

'Please, ma'am,' interrupted the colonel, 'I shall not simply cut him adrift – I shall order him back with a soldier, responsible for seeing that he returns safely. Now, the matter is resolved. Will you all return to your proper quarters.

'Corporal?' called the colonel to a man on sentry duty. 'It is your job to see the boy gets no food. He is allowed water, but nothing else, you understand?'

'Yes, sir.'

As the colonel began to walk away, accompanied by a still-muttering quartermaster, Swinburn suddenly shouted, 'It'll be Privates McSween and Wilson, sir. They'll be the men responsible . . .'

The colonel whirled. 'What?' he said, pulling on the ends of his moustache. 'McSween again? And Wilson? Are you sure, boy? Private Bates, is this true?'

They all stared at Charley, whose expression confirmed what Swinburn had suspected. Charley might have been able to *withhold* the truth, but he could not tell an outright lie. He struggled with his tongue, but nothing came out of his mouth except a strangled noise which could have meant anything.

'I see,' muttered the colonel. 'Well, you two boys go to your tent. I'll speak to you again later. If this is true, you will still have to be punished, Private Bates, for disobeying regulations, even unwittingly. A soldier cannot hide behind the excuse of not knowing or understanding an order. But I will be mindful of your youth and ignorance.

'My earlier punishment of going without rations is to be rescinded, corporal,' he told the duty soldier. 'We shall devise another one in the morning.'

'Sir,' said Swinburn boldly, 'might I also tell you Bates has only been a soldier these past few days. He's still learning. I'm the one who's teaching him, so I should be punished for not showing him well enough how to follow the regulations – I should be punished if anyone should.'

Lieutenant-Colonel Peters' eyes now had an amused glint in them, but he said gravely, 'I shall bear what you say in mind, Private Swinburn.'

With that the two boys went off to their beds.

Lying in the dark of the bell tent, Charley whispered, 'Why did you tell on them?'

Swinburn said fiercely, 'They're a couple of rogues, those two. You ought to stay away from them.' He was quiet for a minute, then added, 'I had to tell – you'd have been discharged from the regiment with dishonour – that's a terrible thing to happen to someone who's not at fault.'

'With dishonour?' whispered Charley, horrified

at the sound of the word. It was as if someone had told him his soul had narrowly escaped going to Hell. Charley shivered at the thought. He wondered if his cousins would ever have spoken to him again if he had been dishonourably discharged.

'Will McSween be dishonoured?'

'Naw, he'll probably be flogged.' Then, as if talking to himself, Swinburn said, 'I'll have to watch my back for a while – that McSween is a villain. He won't enjoy being flogged again so soon after his last time, and when he finds out it's me who gave him away, he'll be as mad as fire.'

'I'll tell him it was me,' said Charley.

'No, he'll find out the truth anyway. Just leave things be. The dust will settle soon enough.'

'Thank you, Swinburn,' said Charley.

'Don't mention it.'

A grumble came from the other side of the tent, where the buglers slept.

'Would you mind shutting up now, you two? I'm to be woken by the sentries at five o'clock to play *reveille*.'

'Sorry, Bangles,' Charley said.

With that the tent fell into silence.

The following morning Charley had to witness McSween's punishment. It was a day when the dew bent the tall grasses with its weight. An early mist sought hiding places in amongst the gorse, and the landscape looked as if it had just emerged dripping from a long sleep at the bottom of a lake. Birds alighted on branches as if they had all been on long journeys to the far corners of the earth.

Private McSween was tied to the wheel of a field gun and flogged. His back took fifteen strokes of the whip. It ran red with blood where the lash opened the skin. He only made one sound, a kind of groan every two or three lashes. Charley found it hard to watch without his eyes stinging. If McSween did not shake, Charley trembled for him.

Swinburn said McSween had got off lightly, for he could have received up to *fifty* lashes.

The boys themselves were ordered to take the officers' chamber pots to the latrines for a week. They had to carry stinking sewage and dump it in a pit. Swinburn was sick every time he did it, but he did not complain, either to Charley or anyone else.

Despite all that had happened, Charley did not feel he could abandon McSween. He went to see him.

McSween was lying on some duckboards on the floor of the tent, his wounds bared to the air. Wilson was busy rubbing balm into his cuts and weals.

'Ho, it's the traitor, is it?' snarled McSween, turning his head away. 'You and that Swinburn. Get a man flogged, would you?'

'You would have had me thrown out of the army,' protested Charley stoutly, 'which is worse than a beating.'

'How would you know?' asked Wilson.

'I've been beaten before. You made me break regulations. You didn't tell me, you just made me break them. That's worse than being a traitor.'

'Ho, is it?' McSween said, his eyes watering as his back smarted after being rubbed by the rough hands of Wilson. 'Is it indeed?'

'I think it is. At least you're still in the army.'

McSween lifted his head and roared, 'You think that's a blamed reward? Bein' in the damned army, boy? Why, there's a thousand other places I'd rather be. There's a thousand other things I could be a-doin' of. The *army*,' he spat. 'You can keep the blamed army and shove it in your dirty washin' bag.'

'I'm sorry you feel that way, McSween, but –

why – only the other day you were telling me how the army would suit me.'

'Suit you, you half-pint – not me.'

Charley sat down on the floor of the tent and watched Wilson ministering to his comrade. McSween occasionally flinched, but he did not cry out, although he was obviously in great pain. He stared moodily out of the tent doorway, ignoring Charley's presence, until Wilson was finished. Then he sat up and gingerly pulled on his grey flannel shirt.

'I've been flogged before,' he grunted, more to himself than the company. 'I can take anything they can dish up.'

'Course you can,' confirmed Wilson. 'You're as tough as old leather, you are.'

'That I be. Takes more than a flogging to upset McSween. I'm just sick to get punishment when I didn't even get a taste of my bob's-worth of liquor. You owe me that bob,' said McSween, turning on Charley again. 'You pay me back my twelve pennies.'

'I'm sorry for it all, but you brought it on yourself, McSween. Swinburn told me so.'

'Did he now,' McSween said, his eyes glinting. 'Well, I might not do nothin' to you, but I'll have that

Swinburn before the war's over, you see if I don't. I'll paint his waggon for him one of these days, when he's least expectin' it.'

'You are a bad man, McSween,' Charley told him. 'If you hurt Swinburn I shall not fetch and carry for you any more.'

'Won't you, you little rabbit,' McSween said, grinning through his pain. 'Well, that would make us think a bit, wouldn't it? Eh, Wilson? No personal slave, eh? Cor, what would cock robin do then, poor thing?'

5 Sailing to Constantinople

When the 1st Battalion of 44th Foot, East Essex Regiment, reached the streets of Portsmouth, they had a reception. As they entered the city they sang 'Cheer, Boys, Cheer', a favourite song of troops. People came to their windows and greeted the soldiers. Women threw their handkerchiefs and men saluted them. Charley felt immensely proud, marching beside Swinburn at the front, and tried to keep to the rhythm set by the other drummers.

'Listen how they cheer,' he said to Swinburn, his boots stamping on the slick cobbles of the street. 'They must like us, mustn't they?'

Swinburn shook his head sadly.

'They cheer us now, but in peacetime they despise us. When we're billeted on towns they kick up a mighty fuss. Soldiers are banned from the inns by the innkeepers and it's a terrible to-do if there are scraps. They want us to fight for the country, but they don't want to see us or have us around.'

Still Charley was like a peacock with a fanned tail. He strutted around, along the harbour, calling hello to the sailors on the ships. He fed the seagulls with crusts he would have eaten himself a week before. He stopped to talk to strollers along the promenade when they expressed curiosity about his regiment.

And Portsmouth was such a bustling place, the harbour full of jostling sailing ships and new sail-steamers. The wharf was like an ants' nest which overflowed with busy people carrying goods here, depositing cargo there. Lighters criss-crossed the harbour, unloading the big wooden ships and carrying their wares to the shore. There stood the owners of the ships, with their waggons ready and waiting to take the goods to markets.

Occasionally there was the crack of sails filling with wind as a ship left port. From the harbour wall, family and friends of the merchant mariners would

59

wave until the vessel was out of sight. First the hull would disappear down behind the curving horizon, then the masts with their sails, one set at a time. The mainsails, the gallants, the royals and finally the little flags on top of the masts. Then it would be lost to sight, down behind the watery slope of the world.

Even more exciting were the men-o'-war, the Royal Navy vessels – battleships and the like – which bristled with cannons. Fighting ships of the line. Some of these would accompany the troopships on which the 'Army of the East', as the British expedition was now known, would be transported to Turkey.

The following day, Charley and Danny were bustled aboard the *Pandora*. They were taken down into the hold and told to find a sleeping space amongst the ropes and other gear stored forward of the hold. They made a little nest for themselves while the rest of the troops poured on to the ship, seeking their own bed spaces. When the boys had established themselves, they went up on deck.

'Do you have a family?' asked Swinburn.

Charley shook his head, a little shy of such matters when talking with another boy. 'Well – my dad's always away – sometimes I see my aunts and uncles.'

'Did they look after you?'

'They've got too many children to look after already.'

Swinburn raised an eyebrow. 'My father said I should join a ship,' he confessed. 'He's in service in Chelmsford. He's a footman even though he's quite old. It's a shame he was never made a butler. My mother's a maid and gets weary easily. She finds me too much to handle.'

'Have you any brothers or sisters?'

'Several, but they're all older than me and in service now.'

'So they didn't mind you going away?'

'They said I should either have to be a boots in some establishment or other, or join the navy.'

'But you're in the *army*,' Charley said.

Swinburn grinned. 'I know – fooled 'em all, didn't I?'

They set sail on the evening tide, gliding out over still waters past the Isle of Wight and the Needles. The lights of Portsmouth glimmered in the dusk. Mariners' brass and glass lamps dangled from the ships, swaying gently as the tide rocked them. These too glowed softly in the mellow twilight. In the air,

61

seabirds wheeled silently, their white-feathered bodies swooping around the sails.

Looking over the rail of the great wooden ship, Charley felt a pang of homesickness for Rochford. This soon passed though, as he remembered the only one who would miss him from that little market town was Sam the dray horse. And dear old Sam was getting old now at nineteen years, so perhaps he would not even be there if Charley ever returned?

His nostalgia was quickly replaced by a terrible seasickness as they entered the Bay of Biscay. Before long, twenty-foot-high waves were lashing at the ship and tossing it about like a cork. Charley's supper went over the side and still his stomach was not satisfied and began reaching ever further down for his breakfast.

'I'm going to die,' he told Swinburn, who was almost as bad. 'Please tell my dad when you see him.'

Swinburn groaned. 'I shan't be seeing anyone – I'm going to die with you.'

Wisely, they stayed up on deck, despite the boisterous seas, huddled in the space under the quarter deck gangway. Salt water foam gushed around, soaking them to the skin. So long as the boys remained jammed under the gangway, they were perfectly safe from being washed overboard.

Down below there were men in much the same state. The hold soon began to stink with vomit. Those who were unaffected by seasickness were organised into bucket chains, to swill out the hold with seawater. The world turned wan for a time, the air hissing with sea spray and white wind. To open one's eyes was an effort in the lashing, stinging spume that came out of the vortex of the storm. Even then nothing could be seen through the salty mist. Down was up and up was down, with the ship boring through troughs into curling walls of water, which reared above then crashed down in tons.

After twenty-four hours the great ship, with its creaking timbers and humming ropes, was carried into calmer waters. The rest of the convoy was there too, previously hidden by the grey waves that had clawed their way up the heavens. Stomachs now began to settle to a mild queasiness.

Accompanying the convoy was a massive steel steamship called the *Caradoc*, which seemed to push the waves aside rather than ride over the them. Charley was fascinated by this iron-clad monster, wondering how it could stay afloat.

'Iron sinks, doesn't it? It's not like wood. Wood floats, that's why ships are normally made of wood,' he said to Swinburn. 'I mean, how can a thing made of so many tons of iron stay afloat? Why doesn't it sink to the bottom?'

'The captain must have a special arrangement with God,' said Swinburn, who was always a little too blasphemous for Charley's comfort.

'No, really, Swinburn – how does it?'

'I don't know,' confessed Swinburn seriously, 'but I once had a copper bowl and *that* floated. So does an iron bucket, so long as it's not too thick. I think it's something to do with the shape of the thing.'

The further south they went, the warmer became the weather. Off came the shirts, to bask in the sun. Flying fish were found on deck one morning. Porpoises were seen arcing through the bow waves. Charley felt lighter and happier as warm winds stroked his skin.

To keep themselves amused, the boys played pranks on the older men. Things came to a head when Swinburn discovered a metal triangle and its striker in the hold. This was the instrument which was sounded to warn of a fire on board. The temptation was too much for Charley, who straight away struck the triangle several times, sending its ringing tones throughout the ship.

Sailors immediately came sweeping down the gangways into the hold.

'Where's the fire?' they yelled. 'Everyone up on deck.'

Soldiers poured up from below, dangerously crowding the upper decks. Two longboats and a cutter were made ready for launching, in case the ship was going down. Men were already jostling for position on these vessels. There was not a panic but it came close to it. When no fire was found, the boys immediately came under suspicion.

This time they were not taken to the colonel, but dragged before the ship's captain, who was lord of all at sea.

'You were responsible for this foolhardy jest?' he cried.

'I'm only ten,' said Charley. 'I didn't know.'

'My cabin boy is but a year older than you and he has more intelligence in his little finger,' boomed the corpulent captain. 'I should have you flogged. Instead you will both oblige me by first climbing the rigging to the crow's nest. You can stay there for the next six hours, after which you will climb down again. Then you may scrub the decks from stem to stern.'

They scrambled up the rigging, at first like monkeys, but then as they got higher and higher, and the deck started to look like a pocketbook below them, they grew more cautious. There were rat lines, buntlines, stays, braces and shrouds to avoid. Soon their legs began shaking. Swinburn was the first to make the crow's nest. He reached down and hauled a shaking Charley in there with him.

'Well, we made it,' cried Swinburn triumphantly. 'I'll wager the captain thought we would fall! Now we just have to stay here for the next few hours . . .'

It was very cold amongst the shrouds. They crouched in the crow's nest, too small to allow them to do more than sit shivering on their haunches. A sharp wind scythed right through them. It was true they had a view out over the vastness of the dark-running sea, but since there was nothing out there except spindrift flying off the white horses, it soon became boring.

They attempted to keep each other's spirits up. They played word-guessing games. They called to the seabirds in the rigging. Swinburn threatened to pee over the edge of the crow's nest, on to the captain's head, but of course did not dare. Talking about such things made it worse for Charley. The cold made him want to go and finally he announced miserably, 'I've wet my trousers.'

'Never mind,' said Swinburn comfortingly, 'they'll soon dry in this wind.'

Down below them was a dizzying drop which made Charley feel sick every time he poked his head over the edge to look. Far below, through the tangle of lines, men were as busy as ants. Later, mariners came swarming up the rigging themselves, and out on to the yards to drop more sail. The boys called to them wearily as the men went out on the foot-ropes, but the sailors were too busy to chat to boys.

As darkness fell, a dispirited Charley said, 'I don't think I'll be playing any more tricks, Swinburn. I can't feel my feet any longer.'

'Nor me mine. My hands are numb too. My shoulders are painful and my bottom hurts. I don't think that captain has any sense of humour. You remember how funny it was with people rushing everywhere – all for nothing.'

Charley knew Swinburn was trying to cheer him up.

'Some people are like that, Swinburn.'

'There's too many folk born without a sense of humour in this world. You can't make 'em laugh, no matter what you do. I once hid in a closet and jumped out on my sister when she opened the door. People said I nearly stopped her heart and killed her,' he said in a disgusted tone. 'I think she fainted on purpose, to get me into trouble.'

Charley laughed. 'Sounds funny to me.'

'Of course it was, but they made such a fuss about it, just because she had a weakness in her chest. If someone blacked their face and jumped out of a cupboard screaming when *I* opened the door, I should think it was a good joke.'

'You blacked your face?'

'So the white bits of my eyes and my teeth were all that anyone could see in the darkness.'

Charley laughed again. 'Jolly funny, Thwinburn,' he said. 'Unbridled hilarity, what thay?'

Both boys screamed with laughter. They were

beginning to pick up mannerisms of speech from the young officers who lounged around the deck smoking cigarettes and playing endless games of cards. Some of these officers lisped purely for effect and the boys were perfect mimics.

When Charley and Danny were finally ordered down from the crow's nest, Charley was suffering from wind chill and Danny from lack of fluid, but a few hours' rest in some warm blankets soon put them back on their feet. A broth was brought to them secretly by the drum major, who didn't believe he was mollycoddling them. It put a bit of strength back into their shivering forms. When they woke they had the decks to scrub. McSween and Wilson had a grand old time, following the boys' progress up the decks.

'Missed a bit here, laddie,' McSween would say, pointing out a dark spot on the planks. 'Better come back and do that one or the captain'll have you keel-hauled, eh?'

Wilson would chuckle at this and then deliberately walk across a drying patch, so that his bootmarks were left visible on the boards.

'Oh dear,' he would say, 'pity about that – don't s'pose you'd care to come back and do it again, would you, Private Swinburn? Or you, Private Bates? S'pect you'll have to when the officer of the watch sees it.'

McSween had not forgiven Swinburn for giving him up to the colonel to save his friend.

'Put your back into it,' he called, 'or that first mate will string you up by your thumbs to the boom.'

'One of these days,' whispered Swinburn to Charley, 'I'm going to take that fellow McSween and give him a sound thrashing – you see if I don't.'

6 The mysterious Orient

When the small British fleet hove into Gibraltar harbour it was a clear and shimmering day. Charley felt as if a golden haze had descended on his life. He and Swinburn, and Bangles the bugler, were leaning over the *Pandora*'s rail, staring out on to the massive rock which was Gibraltar. Fabulous apes gambolled on the top of the island. Down below, in the streets, there were bustling horse-drawn vehicles of every kind.

'Look at it,' said Charley breathlessly. 'A foreign land.'

'More like a foreign lump of stone,' sniffed Bangles, who was older so felt the right to a certain superiority. 'It an't big enough to be a called a land, as such.'

'Well, it's the first I've seen,' Swinburn said, stoutly supporting Charley. 'Those are natives out there.'

'They an't natives,' cried Bangles contemptuously, 'them's Spaniards.'

'Anyone who is native to a land,' remarked Swinburn, whose education was in the hands of the junior officers, 'can be called such. We are natives to Britain . . .'

'You pair of fustilugs,' said Bangles, 'you talk such rot.'

The boys were not allowed to go ashore, but they watched all day from the rail. Local traders came out in small boats to try to sell them goods. Swinburn bought a pocketknife for two pence. Charley purchased a notebook with a lilac fleur-de-lis design on the back and front. It had a royal blue spine, and the paper inside was crisp and white as a sheet of frosty ice on a frozen pond. There were faint decorative etchings of butterflies and birds in the bottom right hand corners of each of its ninety-nine pages. Charley thought it a work of art fit for a king, and it had only cost him a single half-penny.

Bangles said, 'You don't even know how to write – what do you want a notebook for?'

'I like it,' Charley replied emphatically. He was upset by the remark. Later in the day he took the notebook to Dr Porter.

'Could you write my name inside the cover?' he asked. 'Neatly, please.'

'What is your full name, Charley?' asked the surgeon.

He hesitated for a moment before replying, 'Just put "Private C. Bates" if you please, doctor.'

Once the *Caradoc* had taken on coal at Gibraltar, the fleet sailed out into the Mediterranean Sea.

Lieutenant Pickering, bored with the long voyage, wiled away his noons by telling stories. He kept the two boys amused with true tales of many naval battles fought on the Mediterranean to decide the fate of the world in ancient times.

'This is a sea steeped in blood and glory and we are merely passing through its ghosts to another land, where we too will become part of history.'

'Not just blood,' reminded Charley, drinking the knowledge with enthusiasm. 'You said the Mediterranean was thriving with trade too.'

'Oh yes,' replied Pickering, yawning, 'but that's the boring side, isn't it?'

Charley did not think so.

If Charley thought Gibraltar was exotic, he was absolutely astounded by Constantinople. When they arrived at the fantastical city, half of which is in Europe and half in Asia, he was at last allowed to set foot on foreign soil. Once on shore, amongst the colourful Turkish people – whose flowing pantaloons, turbans and brightly coloured shirts and waistcoats made them seem like figures out of a wondrous dream – his fascination was boundless.

The men wore pistols and wicked-looking curved daggers in red sashes wound about their middles. The women were dark-eyed and smelled of musk. The children were mischievous, dirty ragamuffins who would steal the buttons off Charley's coatee if they could.

The inlet was called the Golden Horn. Charley discovered an arcade selling spices, so fragrant you could smell them from half a mile. He saw huge gilt-domed mosques made of blue stone, jade churches and the temples of Suleiman-the-Magnificent. The city bristled with spires and minarets which sparkled in the sun. It seemed as if there were diamonds in the air. There were markets full of mysterious brass objects. It was a world which sent shivers of fear and delight down Charley's spine.

There were also the fly-blown carcasses of dead dogs lying in the street, rubbish and swill overrunning the dirt roads, and diseased, eyeless beggars whose limbs flowed with open sores, but Charley was too overwhelmed to notice this side of the city.

The regiment was sent to Scutari Barracks, up on a hill, which was rife with rats and lice. Charley and Swinburn were given the job of hunting rats, and promised an extra farthing on their pay for every dozen rat tails they produced. They would wait by the rat holes at night, with lumps of wood, to strike the vermin as they crept out. If they missed, the rat would be off squealing, running over the sleeping forms of the men. The two boys would give chase, striking out at random, hitting walls, floor and soldiers who yelled out in protest. Eventually they would corner the rat. If it was a large one and looked too ferocious, the boys let it alone, otherwise they added its tail to their collection. Occasionally, they were bitten.

The men of the regiment got drunk most nights.

'Lend us a few pence,' Wilson asked Charley one evening. 'I'll pay you back on Friday.'

'All right. If McSween will be friends with me again.'

'Oh, I'll make sure of it,' said Wilson, pocketing the five pennies. 'You'll be the best of pals again in no time, you wait and see.'

Swinburn shook his head sadly when Charley told him.

'That's five pennies you won't ever see again. Kiss them goodbye, my friend. You are a poorer but wiser man.'

'He said he would pay me back on Friday.'

'Where money is concerned, such Fridays never come with men like Wilson. At first he will fob you off with promises to repay at a later date. Then he will begin to say that surely he has *already* given you part payment. Finally he will deny all knowledge of the debt. Never lend either of those men any money again, Bates, otherwise you will go home from this war with nothing.'

When McSween asked him for a loan, Charley bluntly refused to part with his money.

'Well,' cried McSween, 'an' there was I thinking you wanted to be pals again.'

'I do,' Charley said.

'Yet you won't lend a good friend a farthin'? It's not as if I'm arskin' for a guinea, or even a crown – a shillin' is all I want to see me through. I need to buy my poor old mum some of them Turkish slippers, to keep her feet warm in the harsh winter time. A shillin's what's being asked, nothing more.'

Charley said, 'Where's your own pay?'

'Gone,' replied McSween sadly. 'Stole from me by some thievin' Turk in a back alley. Held a knife to my throat and demanded my purse . . .'

Swinburn was listening, and he snorted in derision.

'More like the other way round. I bet you've robbed more Turks than you've drunk bottles of rum, McSween.'

Seeing he was getting nowhere with Charley, McSween flew into a rage and chased Swinburn around the barracks. Fortunately the boy could run faster than the soldier, who was hampered by a terrible hangover. Swinburn escaped with his life, leaving McSween gasping and choking for breath, sitting on the stone stairs which led to the courtyard.

'Well done,' said Swinburn to Charley. 'You managed to resist him. You're beginning to turn into a good soldier, Bates. I'm proud of you.'

But Charley was upset that McSween did not like him any more.

The longer they were in Constantinople, the more the boys came to dislike it; the soldiers went from bad to worse. They spent their time drinking and gambling. The officers were little better than the men.

The soldiers' fine uniforms, good enough for a ball when they left England, were beginning to get soiled and dirty. Since they had only one set of clothes – a spare shirt and socks besides – there was little they could do about the situation except attempt to clean the stains. Sergeant-majors despaired, having no smart men under their command any longer.

Some of the officers had large wardrobes and had brought crates of wine and cheeses from Fortnum and Mason. They were attended by their batmen. When they dirtied *their* uniforms, they had new ones made at the Turkish tailors. They walked around resplendent in their gold braid. The bright scabbards of their swords flashed in the sun as they adjusted their jaunty undress caps on their heads and smoked chibouques, long pipes.

Charley wandered the undercover markets of Constantinople, a city that had linked the Bosporus to the Sea of Marmora for two thousand years and more. Ancient Greek triremes had come up from the waters of Hellespont. These were the waters which the great Mede, King Xerxes, had flogged for being stormy when he wanted them calm. In former times it had been called Byzantium. It was a city, full of Greeks, Armenians, Jews, Egyptians, Africans and Indians.

Charley went with Danny one day, deep in to the depths of the suq, a vast covered market, which was a wormery of winding walkways and inner mazes. Charley felt he was in an Aladdin's cave. Every object he saw was a glittering treasure.

'Look at all these things,' he said to Danny. 'I'd like to buy them all. I could sell them in Rochford square and be rich.'

Swinburn's face, dim in the poor light, broke into a grin.

'What would Rochfordites be doing with hubble-bubble pipes?' he said, pointing to the ornate brass hookahs. 'Or silk carpets? Or them fancy curved daggers? Spread out like this it looks like a treasure trove, but you've got to think, Bates, that at home people don't buy stuff they can't use.'

'I like them carved ebony elephants,' whispered Charley, 'and them red-and-gold music boxes that play pretty tunes.'

'I'm sure you do, but I need to go somewhere,' replied Swinburn. 'You stay here. I won't be a minute.'

Swinburn disappeared into the recesses of a stall selling exotic eastern lanterns, but Charley continued to wander until he was thoroughly lost amongst the coffee tents and hookah awnings. He stood for a moment, watching dark faces and light sipping black sludge out of tiny cups, and men with closed eyes sucking water-cooled smoke through silk-covered tubes. He decided to get out into the streets in the open air.

7 Kidnapped by slave traders

'That's a nice bright red coat,' said a voice close to his ear. 'Are you one of the brave soldiers then, protecting this great country from invasion?'

Charley looked up to see a tall, lean man with a hawk-like face. He was dressed in rich flowing robes and a white turban with a yellow jewel on the front. Charley stared at the jewel, which seemed to have a fly trapped inside it. Around the edge was a filigree border wrought in silver.

'Ah,' smiled the man, 'you like my amber brooch?'

'It's a very fine brooch,' agreed Charley. 'What did you say it was? Amber? Is that like a ruby?'

The man laughed. 'No, it is ancient tree-sap turned hard like stone, but it is much prized. If you look along our beaches here in Constantinople you will find many such pieces of amber. Of course, they won't have these nice silver borders – that has to be done later by a silversmith.'

Charlie had seen the street of the silversmiths, and the street of the goldsmiths, with their cracked and chipped saucers of gems just lying in the sun, catching the flashing rays on their facets. It had seemed strange to him that such costly stones should be displayed in dirty crockery. He felt they should be in ornate boxes lined with satin brocade.

'Why's it got that fly in it, sir?' asked Charley.

The man removed the brooch from the front of his turban to give Charley a better look.

'It's not a fly, it's an ancient insect, perhaps thousands of years old. Your own Mr Darwin says they may actually be millions of years old, but I am sceptical. I do not think the world is above four thousand years of age, do you?'

Charlie studied the insect, a creature with long legs and a long pointed nose, with interest.

'I think you're right and the Darwin man is wrong.'

The man with the turban laughed. 'What is your name, boy?'

'Charley Bates – I'm a drummer in the 44th Foot, the East Essex Regiment, sir. I'm getting better at my drum rolls.'

'I'm sure you are, Charley Bates. Here, would you like my little brooch? You may have it, if you come and play for me and my friends. Come, Charley.' The man put an arm round Charley's shoulders. 'Come and show us how to play the drum.'

Charley felt uncomfortable with the man's arm around him, but he did not want to seem impolite. He did not want to take the man's brooch from him either. He wanted to find his own shiny yellow amber on the shores of the Bosporus.

'I'll come and play for you,' said Charley, 'but you must show me where to find the amber.'

'You do not want my brooch?' said the man, raising his eyebrows.

'Well, I might have done, but I want to find lots more pieces so I can sell them in Rochford square when I go home to England. I want to find some pieces without flies in them, so they look nicer.'

His companion laughed again, steering him through the milling crowds.

'People cherish them more for having the fly – they think it makes them rarer.'

'Well, I don't,' Charlie replied emphatically, 'and I don't think Rochford people will. They get enough of dead flies lying on the kitchen windowsills. Mrs Johnson's gruel always has flies in it. You have to pick 'em out.'

'Like weevils, eh?' said the man, conversationally. 'We get weevils in the bread here. It is impossible to keep them out. You get flies in your – what is it – *cruel*?'

'Gruel.'

'Just so.'

Charley felt the pressure of the hand on his back, steering him first through the dark labyrinth of the covered market, whose ceiling was sometimes dirty stained-glass high above their heads, and sometimes just a low canvas roof under which he had to duck. Outside he was led through a series of dark alleys between rococo buildings, many with cupolas on their towers.

'I have to fetch my drum,' Charley reminded the man.

'Oh, not to worry – we have a drum. It's – it's in the room where I am taking you. We are now good friends, you and I, Charley. You are my young brother, eh?'

Charley felt they had not known each other long enough to be talking about being good friends, and they were especially *not* brothers. Many of the local people were like that though. They stopped you outside their goods stalls and said, 'Come in, my good friend. Sit down. You will have lemonade with me, yes, and tell me about your home? The lemonade is free from me, for you must be thirsty. We shall be very, very good friends, yes? Then you will look at my humble wares . . .'

When he glanced up at the man's hawkish features, he saw the dark-brown shining eyes glancing intently around him.

'What's the matter?' asked Charley. 'Is someone after us?'

The man looked a little startled, but then laughed nervously.

'No, no. One has to be careful, young man. These

backstreets are full of robbers and thieves. There are many infidels in Constantinople, who believe in neither the Moslem Koran nor the Christian Bible. They are atheists, who have no God. They would slit a man's throat for his purse.'

'I've got my sword,' said Charley, showing the man his marmaluke.

'Just so,' replied the other, guiding Charley down a very narrow alley which almost touched their shoulders as they walked down single file, Charley in front. 'In here,' murmured the man, pushing Charley a little roughly.

Charley went through a bead curtain into a cool but dirty room where two rough-looking men sat at a table drinking coffee. One of them raised his eyebrows at Charley's tall guide. The other man smiled at Charley through blackened broken teeth. Charley noticed a thin dribble of black coffee running down the corner of the man's chin and dripping on to his waistcoat.

The three men talked in a harsh-sounding tongue. Then the man who had brought Charley to the room turned abruptly on his heel and left. Charley was feeling bewildered.

'When do I play my drum?' he asked the man with the broken teeth. 'Have you got a drum?'

'You – sit down,' said the other man, who wore a red scarf as a belt. 'Sit down – now.'

His English was broken and scarred. Charley felt indignant. Who was this fellow to order him around? He had no rank in the British army.

'I'm going,' said Charley promptly. 'You'd better watch your tongue, sir. I'm a private in the Army of the East.'

Red Sash said something to Broken Teeth and the second man got up and struck Charley a heavy blow on the side of the head. Charley fell to the greasy, wet, stone-flagged floor. He was dazed by the man's fist. He lay there for quite a while. Cockroaches ran over his hands and face. When his head stopped spinning he sat up and brushed off the cockroaches.

'What did you do that for?' he asked miserably. 'Where's my friend gone?'

Red Sash laughed throatily, tearing off a piece of unleavened bread and stuffing it in his mouth.

Spitting crumbs, he said, 'Your friend? He no your friend. We sell you, boy.' He rubbed his forefinger and thumb together. 'We sell you for slave. Get much

87

money for nice little English boy. You come on boat with us.'

'Sell me?' cried Charley, appalled. 'You can't sell me – I'm a soldier.'

The man reached down and took Charley's sword from its scabbard.

'Sell you, or cut you, see?' he made a swishing sound through the air. 'Cut your throat.'

A chill of fear went through Charley. It was not only the threat that worried him so much as something else, something he had not told anyone, not even Swinburn. Once that secret was uncovered, worse things might happen to him. He had to escape.

Charley was kept in the room all day, until darkness fell over the ancient city. Once he thought he heard someone calling his name from the street, but since the two men blocked the only doorway to the room, he could do nothing except yell out. This brought another beating from one of the men. He wept afterwards, but the two thugs had no pity. They simply laughed at his tears.

After dark, when the sounds of barking dogs and distant ships were much clearer, the man in the white robes returned. He said something briefly to his two henchmen in their own tongue. Then he turned and spoke to Charley.

'You have not been a good boy. If you do not behave, we will have to tie you up in a sack and carry you. It will not be pleasant to be in a sack, with your mouth covered and your hands bound. Are you prepared to be good?'

Charley nodded, feeling wretched.

Red Sash and Broken Teeth each took one of his arms. He was frogmarched out of the room and along the street. Hawkface went first, glancing right and left before crossing alleys. Quite soon the smell of the salt water was in Charley's nostrils. There were the cries of gulls. He knew he was being taken down to the waterfront.

Sure enough, when they emerged from the last alley, there was the black water glittering in the light from ships' lamps. Charley did not recognise this part of the harbour. There were no British ships moored here. Only sea-worn wooden Arab dhows and booms, creaking violently as they were pushed against the quays of the waterfront by the lapping of the waves.

'Where are you taking me?' asked Charley, now frightened out of his wits. 'Where are we going?'

'Quiet, boy,' hissed the leader, 'or you will find yourself floating amongst that harbour rubbish before dawn.'

At that moment a man came along one of the jetties with a woman on his arm. Charley saw the flash of gold braid in the light of a hanging lamp. He was certain this was a military man of some kind. Perhaps a sailor going back to his ship out in deep water, begging a ride from one of the owners of the dhows?

'Hey!' cried Charley. 'Help! Help me!'

Broken Teeth struck him hard in the mouth, instantly making his gums bleed.

But the soldier had heard. He dropped the woman's arm and peered into the gloom. At the same time he called out in a language foreign to Charley. Red Sash swiftly reached into his robes and pulled out a pistol.

'Look out!' cried Charley. 'He's got a gun!'

Hawkface said, 'You stupid boy . . .'

There was an explosion close to Charley's ear. Flame seared from the end of the pistol's barrel, lighting the blackness around him. A wooden post halfway down the jetty cracked sharply and sent up chips of wood in a shower. A bright flash came from the end of the jetty, where the soldier stood, followed almost instantly by the sound of a shot. Red Sash let out a scream and staggered backwards clutching his chest. He made some sort of pleading gesture to Hawkface. Then he fell over the edge of the dock into the water. There was a soft splash, a thrashing sound and then silence.

Broken Teeth started to run back down the alley from which they had all come. Charley, now free of any restraints, head-butted Hawkface, who fell backwards, joining his minion in the water.

Charley scampered towards the soldier and his lady. When he glanced back, he saw Hawkface swimming out across the harbour towards a dhow. His flowing robes swirled about him in the water, making his task extremely difficult. Charley saw him haul himself on board the dhow, using the anchor rope. He shook his fist in the direction of Charley, and disappeared below.

Charley turned to see who was his saviour.

'Thank you,' he called to the man, who was advancing towards him.' 'Thank you, sir. Private Charley Bates, sir. Army of the East.'

He saw now that it was a French army officer. He held the silver revolver with which he had shot one of the slavers. He was tall, haughty-looking, and his uniform was magnificent: a single-breasted blue tunic with short and baggy, blue-grey trousers. On his head was a shako with a sweeping black plume that flopped to one side. At his side was a splendid-looking sword with a knuckle-bow hilt.

'Lieutenant Christian Legarre,' said the officer in perfect English, 'of the Imperial Guard – the *Chasseur à Pied* – at your service, young man. You are a drummer boy from one of the foot regiments, are you not? What are you doing in the company of such men as those rogues, child?'

'I was tricked, sir,' said Charley miserably. 'The man who swam to the dhow said he'd help me find some amber.'

'Amber? How novel. I think you almost found yourself a slave in some terrible place.'

The woman came up to them. She was dressed in a red gown and her dark eyes glittered. Though she was clearly not from France she spoke to the officer in French, and he replied. Then he took her arm in his as she turned to flash a wide smile at Charley.

'Come,' said the officer, 'we will escort you to your barracks. Where are you billeted, young man?'

'On the hill, sir – Scutari Barracks.'

'Let us step out then, for I must take this lady back to her lodgings safely afterwards.'

Once in sight of the barracks, Charley suggested he ought to go in on his own. The fact was he was embarrassed at being escorted, thinking that Swinburn would call him a sissy. The lieutenant seemed to understand.

'Be careful in future, boy. Do not believe all you are told by strangers.'

Charley reassured him. Once the officer and his lady had gone, Charley dragged his heels into the barracks and found Swinburn.

'Where have you been?' cried Swinburn. 'We're under orders to sail. Pack your haversack and knapsack straight away. Get 'em on your back. At least you'll be ready when Company-Sergeant Bilford comes to discipline you.'

'Discipline me?' cried Charley. 'What for?'

'For being missing all afternoon, you idiot. We've been drilling and marching, getting ready to go on to the war. You were supposed to be there.

Sergeant Bilford was as angry as a wasp.'

Thoroughly upset by this further turn of events, Charley set about packing his kit. Just then Sergeant Bilford entered the billet.

'Private Bates, did I make a mistake when I took you out of that dirty fly-ridden market square? Did I? Where was you today? Lieutenant Pickering has been on my shoulders since noon, sayin' you had deserted the regiment. "Shoot him," said the lieutenant, "as soon as you clap eyes on him. Shoot him dead before he comes out with more of his wild excuses. Save the execution squad time and money." Well, I'm not as harsh as the lieutenant, so I will listen to an excuse before I takes up my rifle and does what we do to any cowardly deserter from the British army. Well, lad, I'm listening.'

'I was kidnapped,' blurted Charley, 'by slave traders.'

Swinburn who had been standing by, mouth agape, rolled his eyes up into his head.

8 On the Golden Horn

'Kidnapped, was you? By slave traders, was it? I see. You wasn't by chance drinkin' sherbert all afternoon in one of them tents down by the suq, eh? Oh, no, you was kidnapped by nasty slave traders. It happens to British soldiers all the time, don't it?'

Charley suddenly realised how improbable his story sounded and he wisely decided to drop it immediately. It was better to swallow the truth, which could not be proved, and take any punishment that was coming to him.

'I forgot,' he said, hanging his head. 'I forgot there was a parade today. I forgot the time. I'm sorry sergeant – I'll remember in future.'

'Hold your head up, private, you're not a dog are you? Stand up straight. Stand to attention! That's better. Now, I'm going to help you remember in future and you'll thank me for it. You'll be on kitchen fatigues for the next three weeks, whether we're on the ship or on the shore. You understand me? I'd rather shoot you, but the army's a bit particular about wasting ammunition. Now, Swinburn, you make sure this dolt remembers he's on fatigues, 'cause he's likely to forget in his state of mind. See to it.'

'Yes, sergeant,' said Swinburn.

Once the sergeant had gone Swinburn heaved a sigh of relief.

'You got off lightly there, Bates. You really ought to watch what you say. What happened to you after I went to the toilet? I came out and you were gone. I searched everywhere for you.'

'I got lost,' admitted Charley disconsolately. 'I just looked at a few things and when I looked up, I was lost. This man came. He seemed friendly. He took me to a house where he said he would help me find some amber. There were two other men there who hit me and wouldn't let me go.'

Swinburn frowned and stared into Charley's eyes.

'Save all that rubbish for the sergeant, Bates. This is Swinburn you're talking to.'

'I swear to you, Swinburn. Look, I've got cuts and bruises.'

'You've always got cuts and bruises. You collect 'em like some people collect seashells. Come on,' said Swinburn wearily, 'let's get your kit packed. We're due to go on the boat at midnight.'

Charley realised he would not ever be able to convince his friend that he had been kidnapped. He gathered together his belongings and was soon marching with the battalion down to the waterfront. Then they had to wait in a long single-file line to board the rowing boats which would take them out to the ships.

The quays and wharves were very active, with both the British and French armies boarding their vessels. NCOs were walking down the lines, making sure things were orderly. Officers stood in groups and talked quietly, smoking Turkish cigarettes or chibouques. Horses were being led down to the water, their hooves clattering on the quayside cobbles.

A group of French officers passed the line where Charley was standing with Swinburn and Bangles.

Suddenly, Charley recognised one of them as the man who had saved him. He called out, 'Sir! Lieutenant! Imperial Guard officer!'

Swinburn turned around and hissed into his face, 'Are you mad, Bates? You'll be beaten for insubordination. Those are French officers.'

Sergeant Bilford had also heard the cry and he came walking down the line, a frown on his face.

But the officers had stopped and one of them stepped forward and peered down at Charley.

'Ah!' he cried, smiling. 'The little drummer boy!'

Sergeant Bilford came up and slammed to attention, saluting the officer. It was clear from his face that he did not *like* having to salute a French officer, a man he would have been at war with only a few years ago. Sergeant Bilford did not even like saluting officers who were from other British regiments.

'Lieutenant, sir. I apologise for the outburst of my private here. The matter will be dealt with by the proper authorities . . .'

'No, no, you mistake us,' said the lieutenant. 'We are old friends, Charles and I. This evening I shot a rogue dead for trying to abduct this young man, who

I must say was fighting bravely for his honour. Slave traders, sergeant. You understand? It could happen to any soldier.'

'Slave traders?' repeated Sergeant Bilford with a gasp. 'You mean, Bates here *was* being kidnapped?'

'Good word, yes, exactly. Kidnapped. How peculiarly quaint, the English language. There were three ruffians, big fellows, impossible for one man to resist. I shot one of them with my pistol. Another ran off. The third was struck by Charles here, and perhaps the brute would have drowned had he not been able to swim, for the blow took him over the edge of the waterfront and into the waters of the Golden Horn.'

'Is this true?' said the sergeant, in a disbelieving and somewhat bewildered voice.

'Sergeant, I am not in the habit of lying,' snapped the lieutenant. 'I assure you every word is correct.'

Sergeant Bilford straightened his back. 'Sorry, sir. Didn't mean to dispute your honour, sir. Just that it sounds like a very strange story, sir. Bit much to take in all at once, if you know what I mean. Apologies.'

'Your apologies are accepted,' said the lieutenant, clicking his heels. He nodded to Charley. 'It was good to meet you again, Private Bates. I look forward to hearing great things of you on the battlefield. Already I know your courage is of the highest order.'

'Thank – thank you, sir,' whispered Charley.

With that the lieutenant turned on his heel and rejoined his friends. They went off down towards the waterfront, one or two of them looking back at Charley as they chatted.

'Blasted Froggies,' murmured Sergeant Bilford, obviously feeling he had been humiliated in some way. Then he stared down at Charley.

'Well, Bates, it seems I was wrong about you. I'll tell Lieutenant Pickering. He might be inclined to let you off punishment in view of the facts. Just watch it in future. Privates in the British army don't get kidnapped by slave traders – and if they do, they make darned sure they don't get rescued by Frenchies. It's not good for the regiment's pride.'

'Yes, sergeant – no, sergeant.'

'Right then,' the sergeant bellowed. 'Move this line along – there's nothin' more to see here. Come on, shuffle them feet – get them boots moving.'

By one o'clock in the morning the soldiers were all aboard their ships and they set off a little later. Charley was not at all sorry to be rid of

Constantinople, even though it had been such an exciting city, a place the size of which Charley had never seen before. He wondered if London were as big and decided that it could not be.

Sailing away from Constantinople, the lights stretched out into the distance, like a myriad of stars on the ground. Beyond those lights to the east was Asia. Charley had heard it was even bigger than England. There were millions and millions of people there, all of different races, different religions.

Also beating against the wind out of the harbour was an old Arab dhow. It was a pot-bellied craft, with sea-bleached gunwales, rope-worn cleats and a thick canvas sail. It bored through the water rather than skimmed over it. On the deck stood a man in white flowing robes, his hand on one of the salt-white sheets near to the tiller. He was looking out at the ocean. Charley thought how lucky he was not to be the dhow's passenger, on her way to some city in the deserted hinterland of an unmapped quarter of the earth.

'Where are we sailing to?' he asked Swinburn. 'Are we going to the war?'

'Varna. Some place called Varna,' replied

Swinburn disgustedly. 'A little village somewhere on the coast of Bulgaria. Anyway,' he brightened up, 'we're said to be sailing across the Black Sea. I wonder why it's called that, Bates. Do you think it's made of ink?'

'It must be,' answered Charley. 'One of my cousins told me a rhyme once. It went:

> *If all the land was paper,*
> *And all the sea was ink,*
> *And all the trees was bread and cheese,*
> *What would we have to drink?'*

'I've heard that one too. So, we're sailing over a bottle of ink. That won't take long will it, Bates? We'll be at Varna before you know it.'

9 Cholera and cavalry

Varna was a pretty village in Bulgaria on the edge of the Black Sea. There the troops rested again, growing bored. After the heady delights of Constantinople, Varna was a slow, lazy place with little to do but watch the corn ripen in the fields. The soldiers had seen all this sort of thing before. Most of them had been farmhands and they had joined the army to get away from such a dull life.

Charley quite liked it though. There were picturesque orchards and vineyards, with pretty white houses like sugar cubes lying on the landscape. The smell of overripe fruit was in the air, as fruit fermented naturally where it fell. He was pleased that life had slowed down a little after all the excitement.

Unfortunately a terrible disease struck.

'Cholera,' whispered Swinburn to Charley, as if the illness could hear him whisper its name. 'It shrivels you up inside.'

Men began dropping in their tens and dying overnight.

'I'm scared,' said Charley, his eyes round with fear at seeing the corpses laid out in lines on the make-shift parade ground. 'Will we die too, Swinburn?'

No one knew where cholera came from and most of the doctors were convinced it was brought in with foul air. They advised the men to stay away from the stink of bogs, cesspits and the like. They also told them they should eat as much fresh fruit as possible, since this appeared to do good. But they did not warn them off unboiled water.

Danny and Charley, being still young, drank mostly lemonade made from freshly squeezed lemons at a local farmhouse. The water needed to be boiled up with the lemons, which made it safe, though the boys did not know it. In this way they escaped the illness by pure accident.

One day they were out practising their drums in an

orchard north-east of Varna. A troop of horsemen came riding by. They wore the cherry-coloured trousers which earned them the nickname of 'cherrybums', and they were led by a tall, middle-aged brigadier-general who sat poker-straight in his saddle.

'Out of the way, you scamps,' he growled at the boys from behind his grey whiskers. 'You'll frighten my horse with that rat-a-tat-tattin' on them drums.'

They looked up at him to see if he was joking, but could see no signs of humour in his face.

When the cavalry had gone by, Charley said, 'Who was that, Swinburn? Weren't they magnificent? I've never seen such good horses – not even with the gypsies in Rochford market. And the soldiers looked beautiful.'

'That was the 11th Hussars,' whispered Swinburn, also in awe. 'Did you see their sabres? The 17th Lancers are wonderful of course, and the 13th Light Dragoons with their carbines, but the Hussars are the best.'

'Is that the Light Brigade?' asked Charley, staring after the cream of the Army of the East.

'That was them,' confirmed Swinburn, 'and none other than Lord Cardigan himself!'

'Heavens above,' Charley groaned in mock ecstasy. 'The Light Brigade and Lord Cardigan!'

They had seen many wonderful regiments at Varna. There were the Bashi-Bazouks, a Turkish irregular cavalry who wore bright pantaloons, floppy caps and went about bristling with weapons. Many of these men were round and chubby and had long flowing beards, making them look like favourite uncles. But they were fierce and bloody fighters. There were the French Zouaves, also brightly hued, who seemed more African than European in their dress. Amongst the British army, Charley was amazed to see some men wearing skirts. They were big men, who wore pouches in front, and had tall headdresses made of black ostrich feathers.

'Who are they?' he asked Wilson. 'Who are those soldiers in frocks?'

'Them ladies showing their bare knees? Why, they're Highlanders, from the mountains of Scotland,' replied Wilson. 'Jocks, we call 'em. Hunt a creature called a haggis in the heather. Play an instrument that sounds like a strangled cat. Frightens the life out of the enemy. Talk funny too. Their jaws are all gummed up with eatin' stuff called porridge. Can't understand half they say. Them and the Irish. They're always having fist fights between them.'

'You watch your tongue. Don't call 'em *ladies*,' sniffed McSween, 'they're my proud countrymen.'

'You? You've never been to Scotland in your life, you old fake.'

'I've got the blood in my veins,' growled McSween. 'I have the same fighting spirit as the men of the Highland regiments.'

'You'll need it where we're going, son. They say the Russian army is massing on the Crimean peninsula. We're going to have a battle soon – a good old ding-dong. Clean your rifle, McSween. It's going to be used in proper anger.'

'Russians don't frighten me,' muttered McSween, who had just shot a hare for their dinner. 'I can hit a fly on the wall.'

'The trouble is,' said Wilson, more to Charley than McSween, 'there'll be thousands and thousands of flies to hit. Have you ever stood with gritted teeth while the enemy come pouring over the hill, yellin' and screamin' like they was pigs off to the slaughter? I have – we both has, me and McSween. It's a sight that'll have your bones turning to water, boy.'

'I'm not scared,' Charley said, lying. 'I'll just take my sword and defend myself.'

'O' course you will, lad,' cried McSween, laughing. 'You'll hold off a whole column of grey coats, won't you, my boy? Chop 'em down with that marmaluke of yours.'

While at Varna, Charley practised his drumming and soon became very skilled at it. Some of the wives, who travelled as camp followers with the regiments, remarked on how well Charley was doing. He was a favourite with the soldiers' wives and with some of the officers' ladies. Being an apple-faced young boy, they fussed over him. Charley did not like this, but Swinburn encouraged it.

'Bates, you are a fool not to let them pinch your cheeks and call you ducky. We get all our treats from the wives. Why, only the other day we had that pudding steamed by Corporal Turnhouse's wife.'

Charley's brows furrowed and his face darkened.

'I don't want to be treated like a child.'

'But, Bates, you're the closest thing to a child they'll get out here, apart from the local urchins. They're not allowed to bring their children to the battlegrounds.'

'That's not my fault,' grumbled Charley.

'No, but surely you like the treats we get.'

'Sometimes,' said Charley, smiling slyly again. 'I like that toffee Mrs Devlin made for us.'

'Well, there you are then,' Swinburn said. 'Just play along with it. You don't have to enjoy it. Look, here comes Mrs Devlin now, portly woman that she is. If ever one of the ships loses its sails in a storm, all the captain need do is apply to Mrs Devlin for her petticoats and we shall have new cotton gallants and royals to drive the ship along.'

Charley giggled and then Swinburn's voice became louder.

'Hello, Mrs Devlin.'

Mrs Devlin, wife of Private Devlin, swept up to the boys, her large head made seemingly even larger by the tiny mob-cap she wore perched on the bun at the top. She had her skirts held up at both sides to prevent the hems from trailing in the mud, a thing they insisted on doing anyway. A mud-stain reached three inches above her boots and her apron was flecked with brown. Her broad, kind face beamed at them.

'Hello, boys. Did you like the toffee well enough?'

She had an Irish accent which the boys liked for its lilting sound.

'Yes, Mrs Devlin,' they chorused.

'Will you be playin' the drums this mornin', or are we to have some peace?' she laughed.

Charley replied proudly, 'Sergeant Bilford says I've improved beyond measure.'

'Well, I'm sure that's so, Charley. For myself, I'm not too keen on the sound of the drum, for it often means my man marching into battle. Very exciting, I'm sure, for young scallywags like you two, raisin' your din.'

Charley was not so sure he liked his playing to be called a din but he did not argue with Mrs Devlin. At that moment Mrs Duberly passed by on her horse, Bob. She smiled down at the trio.

'Good morning, Mrs Devlin, good morning, boys.'

Mrs Devlin did a little curtsy and murmured, 'Mornin', ma'am. Have you had a good ride?'

Mrs Duberly pouted. 'I was hoping to follow Lord Cardigan's Light Brigade into some action, but they outrode me. They seem to have gone a long way north. Bob and I could not keep up.'

It was well known that Mrs Duberly was fond of battles and would go out of her way to find one. The British cavalry was the most dashing in the world according to her. Her favourites were the Scots Greys of the Heavy Brigade, whose troopers rode tall white horses. 'You can pick them out straight away in any battle,' she would breathe. 'There's no mistaking the beautiful Greys.'

Mrs Duberly left the little group to take Bob to his stable, a rickety shack on the side of a house.

The boys helped Mrs Devlin pick some grapes from the nearby vineyard. The local people were well paid for their goods, since the Army of the East was not allowed to take just what it pleased. Lord Raglan, the commander-in-chief of the British army, insisted that everything was paid for.

Suddenly, McSween came running over in his shirtsleeves and braces.

'We're off!' he called. 'We're sailing. It's to that place called the Crimea. We're to be fighting at last.'

Mrs Devlin went pale. 'Oh, dear God. As if the cholera is not enough . . .'

'But that's what we've come here for,' Swinburn told her. 'To fight. It's exciting.'

'Tell that to me after you've fought your first battle, young man,' she said, walking away.

10 A Crimean landfall

That night Charley boarded a ship again. He was beginning to feel that army life was nothing but sailing from place to place, where one had nothing to do but stand and wait. Still, they said this was different. They said that there was a Russian army on the Crimean peninsula of 35,000 men.

Charley looked round him at the horses being loaded into the ships, some panicking a little and kicking in their traces. Many of the animals had died since leaving England, but then many men and some women had also died. Just *getting* to a war took its toll. Charley thought about life in Rochford, where people froze to death in winter, or starved, or died of similar sicknesses to cholera.

He watched as the guns of the Royal Horse Artillery were hauled on board with ropes and derricks. There were field guns too, howitzers and rockets, and hundreds of round shot and shells in the hold. Charley knew that round shot were solid cannonballs and shells were hollow balls with explosives in them that blew up after being fired, sending hot sharp pieces of jagged metal whizzing through the air. He had only seen them fired in practice and he did not like the noise.

The horses' hooves clattered on the deck as they were hurried past him, their eyes wild with fright at being on an unsteady world that smelled of damp salt.

Swinburn came up beside him. He was in his shirtsleeves, his coatee under his arm. He had been mending a tear with a needle and cotton borrowed from Mrs Devlin.

'What-ho, Bates. On our way at last, eh?'

'Are you pleased to be leaving Varna, Swinburn? I liked it there. We had some good times at our games.' Charley spoke wistfully.

'Good times, yes, but we're off to *war*, Bates.

That's what we came here for. I want to be in the first battle. Look at our fine army! Many regiments of foot, all well drilled and ready for action. Look at all that artillery – why there's even some 32-pounders amongst the naval guns. All these ships too. And the finest cavalry in the world. Then there's the French army, and the Turks. How can we lose against a motley mob of Russians?'

'It's their country, Swinburn. They know it better than we do, and it's their home. Why, if someone wanted to attack Rochford, I would defend it to the last.'

Swinburn snorted. 'It's not *exactly* their country, Bates, not the country of the Russian army. The people who live in the Crimea are Tartars. The Russian army is made up of Russians, Polish troops, and many other foreigners besides.'

'What's the big city called again?'

'Sebastopol.'

Charley looked gloomy. 'I can't even say it,' he grumbled. 'Why are we going to fight in a place I can't even say?'

Dr Porter was passing. He stopped and looked at the boys.

'Because we're British,' he stated. 'We have the British Empire to control. We always fight in places we can't pronounce. We fight and we die in lands that are too hot, too cold, too dusty, too forested – anywhere that's not temperate and comfortable. Deserts, jungles, bush, mountains, wastelands. That's where the British soldier fights and dies.'

'But what for, Dr Porter?' asked Charley.

'For many reasons, I suppose. In this case to stop the Russians from becoming too powerful in Europe. The Russian Czar wants to take over the Ottoman Empire from the Turks. But all wars are different, fought for different reasons.

'Sometimes it's to acquire more lands, enrich ourselves. Sometimes it's for the right to trade; in order to build garrisons and ports in strategic places; to get at food or materials we don't have or grow in England, like rubber and tea, coffee and cotton, rhubarb and china plate . . .'

'Rhubarb and china plate?' laughed Swinburn.

'Oh, you may think that's funny,' said the surgeon, 'and so would I if I knew no different. But we actually fought a war with China because they would not allow us to trade opium for rhubarb – which we did not have in England and thought was a miracle medicine – rhubarb and Chinese crockery. We sent ships up the Pearl River from Hong Kong to Canton, and destroyed the Chinese navy, a fleet of poor wooden junks and sampans.'

'Why didn't they want this opium?' asked Charley.

'Because opium is an evil substance, which destroys the spirit of a man.'

Swinburn said, 'Why did we give them opium if it's evil?'

'They would take nothing at first. So we brought opium from India and traded that instead. In the end the Emperor of China took exception to us poisoning his people and ordered that we should cease trading. The Chinese mandarins destroyed a huge amount of our opium and we went to war.'

After this speech, the doctor walked stiffly away from the boys, as if he did not want to talk further on the subject.

On arrival at the Crimea the *Caradoc* went ahead, sneakily flying a Russian flag at its mast to disguise itself as one of the enemy ships. The people of Sebastopol were amazed to see this great iron ship sail past the mouth of their harbour. Then it cruised up and down the northern coast looking for a good place for the British fleet to use as a landfall and found Calamita Bay where the battalions could disembark.

Charley saw the Crimea emerge out of the mist as he stood on the deck of the *Pandora*. It looked a grim forbidding land. Was this where he was to die? He did not want to go ashore.

A Tartar on an ox-drawn cart paused to watch, until a lone Cossack scout fired a shot from the hills, then galloped away to tell his superiors the enemy had arrived.

Charley clambered down the side nets of the ship into a boat. Already in the boat were a number of Irishmen from the Connaught Rangers. They joshed him and found him a seat down where the water was swilling below the duckboards.

'Sure, there's an infant here, Seamus me boy, not much older than me own son back in County Clare,' said a bearded soldier, smiling down on Charley with broken teeth.

'I'm not an infant,' Charley protested hotly. 'I'm a private in Her Majesty's army.'

'Sure ye are. I'm just joking with ye lad. Don't take on so.'

The other Irishmen laughed but Charley stayed silent, knowing it was useless to make his own retorts. He stared around him at the men, all with beards now, since Lord Raglan had said the men need not shave, overruling General Sir George Brown of the Light Division, who had not approved. In any case, Charley's regiment was in the 3rd Division, which was led by General Sir Richard England, who liked beards.

When the boat bumped against the bottom, Charley jumped out and splashed through the surf to the beach. Once up on the mainland, Charley stared about him as the twilight began to be chased away by the darkness. It was not such a forbidding place after all. There were orchards and vineyards here too. And the odd ghostly farmhouse studding the landscape. It was quiet though, as if the place had been hushed by someone, until he heard the clucking of chickens in a nearby yard, and the snuffle of cows and horses, and the grunt of pigs made him feel less homesick.

Shortly afterwards it began to rain.

11 First shots are fired

The first night on the Crimean peninsula was utterly miserable for Charley and the whole Army of the East. No one seemed to know where the tents were and, in any case, there were no carts to carry them. They might be at the bottom of a hold in some ship, or they might still be at Varna. It meant that they had to spend the night without shelter, bivouacking.

'Here, Bates, help me light a fire,' said Swinburn. 'We need to boil a kettle.'

They were on the steppes, high rippling plains with nothing but low rolling hills to break the view. A chill wind blew in from the north, sweeping over a waving sea of tall grey-green grass. Small birds flew up from beneath his feet as he walked and stared about him at the vast nothingness. He shivered, not so much with the cold, but because the open space scared him.

'Where's the wood, Swinburn? Where shall I fetch the wood from?'

'There's no wood, you clod. We'll have to use grass. Here, do like McSween and Wilson are doing. Tear out the tall dry grass and tie a knot in it. It'll burn slower that way.'

Charley did as he was asked, but the grass still burned too quickly to boil a kettle. Then it started raining. A thin cold drizzle which soaked everyone through to the skin. They gave up their fire and ate a cold meal.

Charley then curled up in his single blanket. He tried to forget the wet, the cold and his hunger. His eyes refused to close and he found himself staring into a dark swirling sky that was not his own. He got up and walked around, sloshing in the puddles. All over the gently rolling landscape there were scarlet-coated soldiers, sitting in huddles, or lying on the wet ground dozing fitfully. 30,000 of them – men who might have to fight at dawn. Others were out on picquet duty, guarding the perimeter. Every so often a shot rang out in the night as some picquet fired his rifle at shadows.

Out in the darkness there could be thousands of Cossacks and Hussars, waiting to charge down on the British camp and destroy it. Or massive columns of Russian infantry, preparing to march into the camp at dawn. They could only imagine what was waiting for them in the dark.

Lord Raglan did not approve of spying. The commander-in-chief had not sent out any forward scouts to find out the size of the enemy army. He did not know where they were or what plans they harboured. Lord Raglan was proud of the fact that he fought his battles fairly. He had been with Wellington at Waterloo, against the French, and had lost one of his arms in a battle. He was more inclined to think the French were still the enemy, not the Russians. Many of his generals thought he was a poor commander-in-chief.

'It's not right to spy,' he told them stiffly. 'Not the done thing at all, gentlemen. Our cavalry can go out in the morning and find out all we need to know.'

The French had managed to bring their tents. The Turkish troops were under canvas too. Only the British had failed to bring the proper equipment to the Crimea.

'Listen to them Froggies, all snoozing away,' grumbled Wilson. 'We only have the uniform we stand up in, and that's fallin' to bits with the dirt and the wet.'

'Stop complainin',' said McSween, 'you never had much better when you was in England.'

Somehow the night managed to drift away. In the morning the rain stopped and a weak September sun came out. Charley's uniform stayed damp most of the day. His bones felt as if they were made of rubber. He had a grisly task to attend to, which kept his mind off his own troubles.

'Seventeen men of the 44th Foot died of the cholera in the night, Bates,' Swinburn said. 'We've got to help carry them to the grave.'

Charley's teeth started chattering. 'Dead men?'

A hand fell on Charley's shoulder and he looked up to see that it belonged to Dr Porter.

'Is it true, doctor? Do I have to?'

'I'm afraid so, Charley. It's a bandsman's duty. In all, over three hundred men perished last night, of cholera and other diseases. The French army have many casualties too. Don't worry, you don't have to dig the grave. The sappers are doing that.'

'I'd rather dig, if you please. I'd rather dig than carry dead men.'

But Charley had to help. However, being so small, in the end all he had to do was carry their personal effects back to their wives or friends.

Most of the women were helping in the temporary hospitals, out in the field or back on the ships. One of them, Mary Seacole, was a West Indian lady who had travelled to the Crimea at her own expense. She took an instant shine to Charley. She told him her name over a cup of tea.

'But everyone calls me Mother Seacole – I'm a doctress, don't you know.'

She told him she had come to the Crimea simply to help the men of those regiments she had known in Jamaica. When she heard there was a call for nurses in the Crimea, she applied to be sent, only to be turned down because of her colour.

'But I'm used to that,' she said, smiling at Charley, 'so I paid my own way.'

Charley could hardly understand her softly spoken

accent, but he understood her smile, and the way she ruffled his hair.

'You're a fine, fine boy,' she laughed. 'You jus' help Mother Seacole do things for the men who is ill. They ain't got nobody else to help 'em – just us few ladies and some small boys.'

Later he heard her say to one of the other wives nursing the men, 'It's a shame the way they send out children to these wars – they should be at home with their mommas.'

Swinburn was covered in dirt and lime by the end of the day. Being larger-framed than Charley, he had been helping to lug the dead-weight bodies. Flies were everywhere in the trenches where they had thrown the corpses. They were caught up in Swinburn's hair and plastered to his sweating face. Still more men died during the day.

There were few ox or donkey carts, as there had been at Varna, so even the officers had to carry their own kit. They had had to leave all their fine wines, hampers and wardrobes on the ships. For the first time in their lives, sons of aristocrats were no better off than their fathers' workers.

Lieutenant Jameson was in charge of the burial

party. He was not one of the rich officers. He was the son of a country parish priest. Unlike most, he had not bought his commission, but had earned it by merit in India. In the officers' mess Jameson was treated with disdain. The lieutenants and captains played tricks on him, like secretly soaking his bed, so it amused him as much as the young boys to see these haughty brother officers sweating like beasts of burden. The cavalry officers had their horses, so they did not suffer as much indignity.

'2,500 years ago,' Jameson told the boys, 'these plains would be thundering under the hooves of Scythian horses. They were horsemen the like of which the world has not seen since. They swept across Asia, even down as far as Egypt, invincible for four centuries – marauders no army could conquer.'

'In-vinc-a-what?' asked Charley.

'*Invincible*. It means they could not be beaten, Private Bates.'

Dr James Barry, one of the chief medical officers, overheard the conversation and spoke as he passed.

'The Scythians also had women warriors, chieftains some of them, charging at the head of their cavalry. Don't forget to tell the boys that, Lieutenant Jameson.'

'Is that true?' asked Charley.

'Yes, it's true,' muttered the lieutenant, wrinkling his nose, 'though why Dr Barry should think that at all significant is beyond me.'

'Chieftains too,' said Charley. 'That means they were officers, doesn't it?'

'Who cares,' Swinburn said, with a little shrug. 'Women can't fight in battles any more – I wager they couldn't do it then – they were probably there to help nurse the wounded.'

'What do you know?' snapped Charley. 'What do you know about Scythians? You only just heard of them, same as I did. You think you know everything, Danny Swinburn. Well, I'm learning some things too, now.'

'Of course you are, Bates,' replied Swinburn, slightly taken aback. 'Of course you are.' He had never seen Charley angry. He put it down to dealing with the sick and dead. No one had told Charley he was to be a medical orderly when he had first joined. When he had taken the Queen's shilling all that had been in his head was a picture of himself in that beautiful red coatee with the white bands. He had felt the power of command in his sticks as they tapped the taut drumskin, telling a thousand men the speed at which they were to march. *Drummer boy*! That had a commanding ring about it. *Medical orderly*, did not.

Later the boys had to help dig a huge latrine, downwind of the camp. It was arduous work, supervised by grumpy NCOs who wanted to be at the field canteen.

The tents did not arrive that day either, or the next day, or the next. Swinburn was convinced they were going to fight the whole war without ever going under shelter again. September was bad enough when you had no other clothes to change into, but the winter would be arriving soon, and it would be as cold, if not colder, than a winter back in Britain.

'They say it will all be over after the first battle and we can go home for Christmas,' said Charley.

Swinburn said, 'I think that's true.'

The boys were sitting up on a rise, looking down on the red ants in the British camp and the blue ants in the French camp – soldiers all busying themselves with cooking a meal or washing socks. McSween had climbed up there with them and he was lying back amongst the wildflowers, his coatee unbuttoned and a piece of grass dangling from his mouth. He looked as contented as McSween ever could.

'They always say it'll be over after the first battle, but I an't been in a war yet which only had one battle.'

The wind rustled through the wild herbs, offering fragrances to the three soldiers. Somewhere near, a game bird was clucking from its nest of hay. A hawk hung above a knoll, its wings beating rapidly, keeping it suspended there. The world seemed so peaceful up on the gentle heights.

The three had unwisely wandered out beyond their own picquets, but no one had seen a Russian since the first landing, so discipline was a little lax. Some of the nearby picquets, 93rd Sutherland Highlanders, were sunning themselves in the warm air.

Suddenly, McSween sat up and stiffened. He looked around quickly. The two boys could see he was alarmed and it worried them. Then McSween's eyes opened a little wider. He put a finger to his lips, indicating that they should be quiet. He waved his hand in a downward motion. Swinburn flattened himself, hiding down in the tall grass. Charley seeing

128

this, copied him. McSween was already concealed.

Charley lifted his head slightly and looked in the direction in which McSween had been facing. He saw a sight which made his heart beat faster. There were three men in loose blue uniforms on horseback. The French wore blue, but these were not Frenchmen. These had long straggly moustaches and unkempt hair sticking out from underneath round furry hats.

Charley knew at once that these were Cossacks. He had heard so much talk about them in the camp. There were the stocky, thick-limbed horses. There were the long lances, the sabres and the carbines on a shoulder strap. Their faces were weathered, with narrowed crinkly eyes set wide apart. They looked hard, tough men.

Charley was glad that McSween was not drunk, as he might have been, or he would certainly have tried to shoot one of the Cossacks. Fortunately the Cossacks had not seen them. They were busy staring down on the British, French and Turkish encampments. Then they must have been seen from below by the picquets, who let loose a ragged hail of shots. This was followed by a loud *halloo*, coming from the area where the Light Brigade was camped.

Some of the 13th Light Dragoons, already on horseback, came charging up the hill. More shots were fired and the Cossacks took flight.

McSween jumped up as the blue-coated warriors fled. He loaded his rifle in seventeen seconds flat, and managed to fire a single round at the retreating Cossacks. They were too far away even for a good shot. McSween cursed at having missed them.

'Nearly got meself some extra pay there, I'll wager,' said McSween. 'You'll tell the sergeant I did my best, lads?'

'We will,' cried Charley, thoroughly stunned and awed by the whole event. 'Oh we surely will, McSween.'

12 Battle of the Alma

Not long after the incident in the hills, the British, with their French and Turkish allies, began the march south. The Russian army had been sighted on the other side of the Bulganak River, which turned out to be not much more than a dirty little stream.

Charley found himself marching in front of his battalion, beating his drum with enthusiasm. The bands made quite a stir amongst the local people, although the British musicians were not quite as colourful and rousing as the French. Passing Tartars on their waggons and carts stopped to stare as the red and blue troops tramped by them en masse.

'It doesn't matter where you live, lad,' Dr Porter

told Charley, as he walked beside him during a lull in his playing. 'People are much the same everywhere.'

'But aren't we the best, Dr Porter?' said Charley, surprised.

'We like to think so, just as the French, Turks and indeed the Russians think they are the best, but happily we are all very much the same. There's good and bad Russians, just as there are good and bad Englishmen.'

When Charley reached the Bulganak there was a skirmish between the two enemy cavalries. He was a little surprised to learn the British got the worst of it. But the incident was a small affair in which the British Light Brigade failed to catch the swifter Russian cavalry during a chase into the hills. General Cardigan's lot came in for a bit of a ribbing for that, which made the noble lord fume in his boots for a few days.

Some worn-out bell tents, left over from the last war, arrived at last. Charley and Danny helped set them up in long lines, then went into one to sleep. It was the first time the boys had been under cover since the landing.

At the Bulganak, Lord Raglan and the French commander, Marshal St Arnaud, discussed their strategy for the coming battle and what the Russian commander-in-chief, Prince Menshikov, might do. Marshal St Arnaud told Lord Raglan *his* plans and Lord Raglan murmured something which *might* have been an agreement. The Marshal was very ill and Lord Raglan thought it best to say something, anything, so that the Marshal could go back to his tent and rest.

So, the next day, on the 20th September, 1854, there was a march down to the River Alma further south than the Bulganak. There in the hills, on the other side of the river, waited the Russian Army which had nearly 40,000 men. Charley's army had nearly 65,000 men, but they were at a grave disadvantage. To attack the Russian army and field gun emplacements, first they had to cross a river under fire, then climb a steep slope to reach the enemy. The Russians could hide behind barriers up on the ridges and hills and just rattle bullets down on the British, French and Turkish troops as they struggled up.

The march south to the Alma was in grand formation, with the British in rectangles and the French in a lozenge shape on their left. First came the Rifle Brigade, then the Light Division and 2nd

Division, side by side. The 1st Division and Charley's 3rd Division followed, then the 4th Division and the baggage train. Finally, to the far left and to the rear was the cavalry, to protect against sudden attack.

Charley felt immensely proud. He had washed most of the mud off his uniform in the Bulganak River and felt he looked as smart as could be under the circumstances. He marched next to Swinburn, who also looked very dignified. Over 60,000 pairs of feet marched with them to the sound of the drums and the music of the fifes, tramping noisily over the Crimean landscape.

Up in front of the marching army, which stretched right across a whole plain, ran the rabbits and hares, the mice and other mammals, all scurrying out of the way of this great monster with thousands of boots. Game birds flew whirring into the air. The scents of crushed wild herbs and shrubs were wafted into Charley's nostrils. Behind them they left the grasses trampled flat.

Occasionally sick men fell to the ground. They were gathered up by the baggage train. Some of their ox carts had been set aside as field ambulances.

Soon the heights of the Alma came into sight.

Now everyone, including Charley, got a queasy feeling in the pits of their stomachs. Little grey dots began to appear on the hills above the river, standing around black muzzles of big guns. Behind these were the mighty columns of Russian soldiers, big blocks of them, bristling with bayonets. They looked like lumbering grey beasts, waiting patiently.

'Is that them?' whispered Charley, suddenly wishing he were back in Rochford square. 'Is that the Russians?'

Swinburn swallowed hard. 'That's them, Charley.'

There was an astonishing sight up on the hill.

In the heart of their defences, the Russians had built a huge wooden viewing platform with rows of seats. This structure overlooked the battlefield from just behind the Russian guns. Sitting in composed lines were the fine ladies of Sebastopol. They were dressed in pretty frilly gowns, their lace gloves in their laps. They twirled lilac, pink and white parasols on their shoulders. Their pert little hats were perched high on their coiffured heads.

Not only Charley was amazed by the sight. The whole of the British army was stunned. No one could imagine what they were doing there.

Suddenly a black dot left the hills in a puff of smoke and came hurtling towards Charley's battalion. It seemed to come as slowly as a cricket ball curving through the air. The closer it got the bigger it became, until it hit the ground in front of the British army and bounced straight at them.

Men quickly scurried aside. McSween grabbed a gaping Charley by the collar and wrenched him out of the way as the cannonball went thumping by, leaving great dents in the ground where it hit. The round shot passed through the whole army without hitting anyone. A great jeer went up, directed at the Russian gunners, who thought they had scored a direct hit. 'What a rotten bowler. Couldn't hit the stumps for trying.'

A few minutes later, as the allied army marched closer, the cannonballs started raining down on them. So did the shells, exploding above them with a noise that deafened all around. Rockets began whizzing through the air. The allied guns returned the fire, filling the air with the terrible noise of battle. The acrid smell of gunpowder attacked Charley's nostrils. His mind rocked and spun with the racket. He had never been so terrified in all his life.

A horse artillery battery came thundering up beside him to unlimber and begin firing their howitzer. The gun was going off repeatedly, BANG, BANG, BANG, BANG, BANG, right by Charley's ear. With each thumping explosion, hot air seemed to slam into the side of Charley's head. He wanted to run and bury himself deep under a pile of blankets.

Cannonballs fell amongst groups of British soldiers. Casualties began to mount as some were killed and others were injured. Pack animals were struck. Carts were smashed to matchwood.

Infantry officers of senior rank went into battle on horseback. They rode up and down appealing for calm amongst the soldiers. Bandsmen were hard at work now, carrying the wounded back to the baggage train, ministering to those who were in need of medical assistance. There was not a lot they could do but offer water and comfort and perhaps act as a crutch where needed.

A water bottle was thrust into Charley's hand.

'Go and give water to the wounded,' said Sergeant Bilford. 'Keep busy, lad.'

The world around Charley was full of metal insects, deadly insects, zinging, whining, humming through the air. It was as if he were in the middle of some raging hailstorm, but the hailstones were made of sharp pieces of iron. Thunderbolts exploded with a crash and roar of flame overhead. Great round balls of iron fell from the sky, their impact making the earth judder beneath his feet. There were cries and yells, booms and blasts, which rocked his small body from side to side.

Charley swallowed hard and took a bottle with trembling hands. He did not know where to start. There were men crying out from all around. He looked at Swinburn wide-eyed, hoping for some sort of leadership. Swinburn who was very pale now, also had a bottle of water in his hands.

'Come on then, Bates,' he said after a moment. 'Those poor chaps need us.'

The grand order of march had been rearranged by the busy generals. The British attacking force now consisted of a long line, two men deep, snaking like a red ribbon right along the valley. Stretched out over the countryside, the whole line of scarlet coats was two miles wide.

Behind this first thin red line was another one the same length. This was the line in which Charley's regiment was standing, waiting to follow behind the first attacking ribbon. Charley was running up and down the line, giving water to those who had been wounded by exploding shells or cannonballs.

When they marched forward into battle, they would not run, nor even go at a fast pace. If they did, the lines might break up and overlap, and there would be chaos. British soldiers would be firing into the backs of other British soldiers.

So they had to march resolutely forward, keeping the line straight. The advantage of this form of attack was that it made it difficult for the Russian gunners to aim at them. Often the round shot and shells went screaming over the line of British soldiers, or they dropped too short of the line to do any damage.

On the other side, the Russians fought in their huge, packed rectangles of several thousand men. They were amazed at the way the British attacked in such thin lines. They thought the British officers would have trouble keeping discipline. They felt sure the red coats would turn and run once they came face to face with the grey masses of Russian soldiers, who were like giant square porcupines with their muskets protruding.

As Charley was trying to help a wounded soldier drink some water, he heard the order to go forward.

The British line began to advance.

Out in front were a thousand or so green coats of the Rifle Brigade – the sharpshooters – skirmishing out in ragged order like little green ants worrying the enemy.

Charley stood and watched open-mouthed.

Straight towards the River Alma marched the twelve battalions, bullets whizzing into their ranks, cannons firing at them from the Russian redoubts up on the heights. Not a man paused in his step unless he was struck by a missile. The courage of these farm boys in uniform was truly amazing. If the line was not straight it was because of obstacles in their path, not because a man failed to go forward.

Through an orchard they went, which hummed and sang with the whine of musketballs. When they reached a low drystone wall, they waited there for a minute to get the line straight again, before climbing over. Down, down a gentle slope towards the river, the surface pockmarked with striking bullets.

Swinburn came up alongside Charley.

'Look at them attack, Charley . . .'

Charley did not need to be told. He was numb with shock. He himself was in danger from the cannonballs falling all around. A round shot landed not ten yards away. It sprayed dirt and stones which stung his face. Charley's heart fluttered in panic. He was close to tears. His legs shook violently. He turned to run, crying out his dead mother's name. Swinburn saw how terrified he was and responded quickly. He ran after Charley, caught him and held him close in a bear hug.

'Don't run, Charley,' he whispered. 'Don't run, for pity's sake. Your name will be posted up in your parish church and you'll be called a coward. Please don't run.'

Charley struggled.

The air around him was hot with bits of flying metal.

Russian gunners and marksmen were blazing away from every part of the hills. Britons were falling in the line ahead, hit by musketballs. When a man fell, the line closed up, so the Russians were not given the satisfaction of seeing gaps. What they saw was a complete line, marching determinedly onwards, towards *them*.

Soon the line reached the river and the regiments waded across the fast-flowing water, many of them falling in the water, their bodies to be swept away and round the next bend.

'Let me go, Swinburn,' cried Charley. 'I want to go home.'

'You can't. You'll be punished very badly. Stay with me, Bates. I'm scared too. I'm so scared my knees are cracking together. But there'll be the devil to pay if we desert the battlefield.'

He let Charley out of the close embrace, but kept hold of his sleeve, placing the water bottle back in his hand.

'Come on, Bates, we're needed here. We have to give those men water. It's all that salt beef, and the hot weather – everyone's thirsty, especially the wounded.'

Many of the men in the battalions that were crossing the river had grapes dangling from their mouths. They were so thirsty that they had picked bunches when passing through a vineyard, even though they had been under fire.

On the right of the Light Division, the 2nd Division were being hampered by houses on fire. The Russians had set light to a village which had been in their path and the heat from the flames was fierce.

Charley obeyed Swinburn, blindly walking forward into the battle area, giving each injured man a few gulps of water. Some cried out to him for more. Others simply groaned and stared. A few kept a stiff and horrible grey silence.

The Rifle Brigade's skirmishers were now pouring up the slopes on the other side of the river. Soon the red line of the foot regiments was marching up behind them. The great grey columns of the Russians trudged forward. They met the narrow line of scarlet soldiers, only to be driven back by the fierce volleys from the superior British Minié rifles.

Many of the Russian soldiers were peasants, forced to leave their homes on the great plains to join the army. They were still armed with old-fashioned muskets. These were such poor weapons that when trodden on they snapped in half like a brittle stick. The British soldiers were all volunteers and their rifles were powerful and accurate, which gave them great heart as they faced the grey massed regiments of Russians.

Charley saw the 19th and 23rd Foot —

Yorkshiremen and Welshmen – swarm over a large Russian gun redoubt. The guns stopped firing from that area. A ragged cheer went up.

It was time to send a second line of British soldiers at the enemy.

The 1st Division was ordered to advance. It consisted of the three crack regiments of kilted Scottish Highlanders and the magnificent regiments of the Guards. The Highlanders wore high hats made of black waving ostrich plumes. The Guards wore huge bearskins on their heads. The men in both brigades looked seven feet tall to the awed Russians. The bare knees of the Highlanders under their swishing kilts frightened the enemy out of their wits. The haughty-looking Guards appeared so arrogantly confident those Russians facing them were already preparing to retreat.

When the Highlanders and Guards swept up the hill the enemy lost heart. Their massive columns let out a wail like that of a wounded beast. They began retreating back down the road behind them to the city of Sebastopol. The British soldiers cheered, their shouts and trumpets filling the air with the sounds of victory.

The noise of battle – the constant din of the guns, the cries of men, the scream of horses, the hail of musket and rifle fire – was all around Charley. Great black clouds of smoke drifted across the battlefield. The pungent smell made Charley's eyes water and his nostrils burn.

The enemy had begun their retreat, but they still turned and fired, and many of their guns had not been silenced. The mangled corpses, the dead and dying soldiers were a nightmare sight to Charley.

A pink parasol went floating by on a wave of hot air.

The Russian ladies had their skirts bunched in their hands as they ran down the back road. Hats flew from their heads. Discarded fans and parasols drifted over the darkened battlefield. The sweet perfumes of the ladies mingled with the harsh smell of gunpowder to form a strange mixture which might have come from a mingling of heaven and hell.

13 Charley refuses to fight

On the other side of the battlefield, the French had also been victorious. The toot-toot-tooting of their trumpets could be heard out at sea, where the fleet of British and French ships awaited the outcome of the battle. The Russians were in full retreat now, pouring over the landscape and down towards the safety of the defences in Sebastopol.

The British generals had failed to give proper orders throughout the whole conflict. It was the officers and men of the line who had won the day. They had used their initiative and despite poor leadership had come through victorious.

For Charley, however, the ordeal was not over.

He was given more bottles of water and told to wander over the heights. If a man called for sustenance, he was to give it. Charley looked round for Swinburn, but could not see him anywhere.

'You'll need to start doing things on your own, Private Bates,' said Sergeant Bilford, not unsympathetically. 'You can't always rely on Swinburn to be with you.'

'Yes, sergeant,' croaked Charley. 'But where is he?'

The sergeant looked vaguely out over the smoky battle area.

'Oh, giving water, somewhere, no doubt.'

Charley climbed the hill up to the heights. The wooden platform on which the ladies had sat was now leaning precariously. A supporting post on one side had been shattered by a British cannonball. Banners and bunting fluttered from the awning like tethered ghosts.

On the way up Charley passed dead and dying men. He gave water where he could. A Russian corporal with a grey and grizzled face lay in a pit. He looked in great pain. Charley could see bullet holes in the man's thick greatcoat. The man called out to

Charley. The drummer boy stopped and stared, then climbed down into the hollow. He pressed the water bottle to the parched, cracked lips of the Russian soldier.

The corporal lapped the water, then stared at Charley with blue penetrating eyes. Suddenly, the soldier smiled. He said something in that strange tongue of his and reached up to stroke Charley's hair.

'It's all right, sir,' said Charley. 'You'll be all right, I think.'

The soldier let out a heavy sigh.

'*Da*,' he said, but then turned his face away.

Charley had to leave him. He climbed out of the pit on to the top of the heights. There were bodies scattered over the plain. Thousands of them. Mostly they were in grey. Only a few hundred were in red or green.

Charley wandered through the black clouds of smoke, doing what he could to make his comrades comfortable. Other bandsmen, other soldiers, were doing the same. The British wives were also there to help. Some simply drifted from corpse to corpse, perhaps looking for a husband amongst the dead. Occasionally a wail went up which meant they had found him.

At one point Charley came face to face with a young girl in pretty ribbons and bows. He was so shocked he dropped his water bottle. Fortunately, being made of wood and metal, it did not break. However, some of the water glugged out on to the ground. The girl tutted.

'Clumsy boy,' she said in a thick accent. 'You waste the water.'

Charley quickly retrieved his flask.

'Are you a Russian?' asked Charley, still amazed at the presence of this girl, who was a year or two older than him at the most. 'Were you on the platform?'

'I help my people,' said the girl, tearing the hem off the bottom of her skirts to use as a bandage. 'Many of our soldiers are hurt. I must assist them. Here, give me the water for one moment, please.'

Charley handed over his bottle and unslung another from his shoulder. He watched as she gave a drink to one of the wounded Russian soldiers. She wiped his brow with a cool hand. Then she did her best to staunch his bleeding with her home-made bandage. She seemed completely in control.

Charley looked covetously at a pretty blue satin

sash, threaded through her white dress. He had never had a satin ribbon like that.

'What's your name?' he asked. 'Mine's Bates.'

'Dasha Aleksandrovna. My father was a sailor, but he was killed. Now, are you going to stand there – or will you help your people? There are many still calling for your water.'

Charley watched as she floated off, like an angel from a dream, going from injured man to injured man. Shots rang out over the battlefield, so she was in danger. Die-hard Russians were ambushing British and French soldiers. Allied troops were still routing pockets of the enemy. Yet Dasha Aleksandrovna seemed oblivious of it all.

Charley wanted to talk to her again, but could not find her. It was dusk now and the sky was turning a murky yellow colour. Soon the darkness would descend. Charley was desperately tired. He wanted to lie down where he was, except that he was terrified of sleeping amongst dead men.

He trudged back the way he had come, towards the edge of the heights, where they fell down to the river. There were large black birds and other scavengers on the battlefield now. He did not want to see what they were doing. Soldiers and women were wandering down the winding paths to the river. Charley followed, crossing over a narrow stretch of shallows. Once on the other side he went in search of his regiment. He needed to speak to Swinburn before he fell asleep. He had to talk about what had happened. Somehow Charley knew that if he did not talk, he would be haunted by bad dreams.

Night fell swiftly as he wandered back to where the Army of the East had a make-shift camp.

'Please, do you know where the 44th Foot are?' he asked a lance-corporal of the Scots Fusiliers, as he stumbled around in the darkness. 'I can't find them.'

'Ye'll no find them the night, laddie,' said the soldier sympathetically. 'It's aye dark and naebody kens where tae find ay-thing. Best ye settle where ye stand, till the morn's morn.'

Charley barely understood but got the gist of what the Scotsman was saying. As he settled down on a grassy patch under a waggon, he thought vaguely that he might be posted as a deserter if he did not report back as soon as it was light.

It was a strange and eerie feeling, sleeping in

silence at night where there had been so much clamour during the day. Charley woke in the early hours. His head still ached from the crashing of the guns and the smell of gunsmoke. He still had visions in his mind of soldiers falling from the line, dropping down into the grasses, dead. Somewhere out in the night came the cold, hollow barking of a fox. Charley shivered and then drowned again in a deep sleep.

When he woke, the heavens were red and angry-looking. Charley got up and drank from one of his bottles. He stared out from under the waggon at the area before the river. It was littered with thousands of shiny shakos and kettles, discarded by soldiers during their advance on the Alma. The British uniform was not for a fighting man; it was made for parades and strutting through parks. It was too tight, too bright and too fancy.

'Guid morning,' said the lance-corporal who had spoken to him the night before. 'Would ye like a knot of salt beef?'

Charley gratefully accepted the breakfast, then thanked him before going to look for his regiment. After searching for an hour, he found them. To his astonishment Charley discovered that not all the

152

wounded had been brought in. He followed Bangles out with water bottles to the battlefield.

The regiment's wives and some of the less battle-weary soldiers had gone out and put blankets over most of the wounded to keep them warm. Charley went from man to man, offering his bottles, upset to find some of them already dead. Finally he came to a shell hole in which a small shape huddled in a blanket. He recognised the dark hair.

'Swinburn?' he said, with a lump in his throat. 'Is that you?'

A feeble sound came from the boy in the blanket.

Charley went to him. Danny's face was ashen, his lips drained of blood. His eyes were half-closed and his breathing very shallow. When Charley leaned over him, Swinburn stirred slightly and shivered.

'It's me – Bates,' said Charley, whose mouth was now as parched as dust. 'Can I give you some water?'

Swinburn's eyes opened a little more. 'You're – you've got the sun behind you,' he whispered in a voice like dry leaves rustling in the breeze. 'Move – move over a little.'

Charley went to one side and Swinburn's eyes followed him. A little smile came to the wounded drummer boy's mouth. For a moment the colour seemed to return to Swinburn's cheeks, but then it faded again quickly. A small sigh left his pinched lips. Finally he nodded, closing his eyes. After a long while he spoke again, even more faintly than before, his breath hardly moving the dust.

'Now I can see you. Now I can see your face – you look fine, Bates, old man.'

'But – but you've got your eyes closed, Swinburn.'

Swinburn did not reply this time and Charley could see that the smile was now frozen to his features.

'Oh, Swinburn. Speak to me. What is it? Are you hurt badly? Help!' Charley cried. 'Someone come and help!'

Charley shook Swinburn, but he did not waken. Charley stood up, his heart racing. Grief flooded into him but he turned it away. Swinburn couldn't be dead. Not Swinburn, who was always bubbling over with plans and schemes.

Charley ran to find someone who could wake Swinburn and make him laugh again.

He found Sergeant Bilford grumbling to his corporals.

'We should have chased after them Ruskies

yesterday, when they was on the retreat. But the blasted Frenchies had left all their knapsacks behind them and wouldn't go on without fetching them. Now them Ruskies has got well away. We'll need another full-blooded battle to bring 'em to heel.'

'Please, sergeant,' said Charley desperately, 'can you come and look at Swinburn – he – he won't move . . .'

'Swinburn?' repeated the sergeant frowning. 'Where is that boy now? I've sent Wilson and McSween and some others to round people up. We'll find your precious Swinburn for you, don't you worry, lad.'

'No, you don't understand,' Charley almost shouted at the sergeant. 'He's not moving.'

At that moment a man came stumbling out of the red dawn. In his arms was a body, carried like a sleeping child. When he came closer and the glare of the morning sun was not so intense, they could see it was McSween. His face had a long and tragic look about it. He reached the spot where Charley and Sergeant Bilford were standing. He laid the body carefully on the grass.

'It's that little tyke, Swinburn,' said McSween in

a choked voice. 'Many's the time I wanted to clip his ear for him. Now he's gone and got himself killed.'

Charley let out a shriek of horror.

'He's not dead. He's not. I spoke to him just a minute ago. Look – look – just wake him up, McSween.'

Charley fell to his knees by the body.

Swinburn's face was as pale as lily petals. His eyes were closed. A black lock of hair now flopped down over one cheek. There were no marks on his body. He was perfect. It was as if the air had been simply sucked from his lungs. Charley would have to face the horrors of war alone.

'Oh, Swinburn, you shouldn't have gone and left me.'

McSween and the sergeant stood there awkwardly, looking down on both the boys, then the sergeant gently urged Charley to get off his knees.

'Come on, lad. You can't do nothing for your friend now. He's gone an' that's the truth of it. Many soldiers died yesterday. This is war. You'll never be a man if you don't learn to bear these misfortunes . . .'

Charley had had enough of the army and its wars. The glory of war which he had been promised was not there. If men did not die of sickness on the march, or of wounds on the battlefield, they died in the field hospitals later.

'I don't want to be a man,' Charley wept. 'I want to go home to Rochford.'

'No, no, you're a drummer boy now, and here's where you must stay. The army's your family, Private Bates. You can't go runnin' off back to where you come from till you're discharged from the army in a right and proper fashion. Till then you must learn a bit of discipline, lad.'

'No, no, no, no,' yelled Charley into the face of a shocked Sergeant Bilford. 'I'm not going to, I'm not going to. I'm going home, you hear me? You have to let me go, you pig.'

Dr Porter and Mrs Duberly overheard what was said. Mrs Duberly glanced at Charley, who gave her a beseeching look. She took the doctor's arm and led him to where the sergeant was still demanding that Charley 'act like a soldier'.

'Just a minute, please, sergeant,' said Mrs Duberly. 'May I have a word with Charley?'

Sergeant Bilford looked a bit put out. It was none of her business but Mrs Duberly was a very strong character, as well as being the wife of an officer, and he finally stepped aside.

Mrs Duberly bent over, took Charley's hand and smiled.

'I want you to come to my room and talk to me, Charley. Will you do that? We'll talk about Swinburn and what's to be done now. Come along.'

Charley allowed her to lead him away, while Sergeant Bilford and the others watched them go in silence.

14 The thin red line

Charley grieved for Danny Swinburn as if the dead drummer boy had been his brother. In many ways he *had* served as an older brother, looking out for Charley, making sure he knew what to do and when to do it. This was really the only way to survive in the army, by having someone wiser to guide you.

He had helped Charley not to look a fool and to know what he was doing when asked to run an errand. He had been near enough in age to be a friend, too.

Mrs Duberly saw to it that Swinburn had a proper grave, which Charley could visit. Charley picked wild flowers and placed them under the wooden cross, which McSween had fashioned with his own hands.

Something of Charley's love for the army had been lost now that Swinburn had gone. His family was not complete any longer. Swinburn was missing from the campfire. Now it seemed an empty kind of life.

Charley decided, while standing at Swinburn's grave, that he wanted to leave the army. He knew he helped by giving water to the wounded on the battlefield, but he could not stand the sight and sound of men shooting each other to pieces, blowing each other up, stabbing each other with their sharp weapons. He was sickened by the whole business of war and wished there could be an army without it.

After the Battle of Alma, the Army of the East marched down past the city of Sebastopol, to a harbour town known as Balaclava They took possession of it. There they remained for some days, laying siege to Sebastopol, which was just to the north west.

Charley was helping McSween, who had reported sick with a slight fever and had been put on light duties with other walking wounded. They were doing some chores around the town, carrying blankets from the wharf to a warehouse.

'The army would be a fine place to spend one's

life,' Charley told an incredulous McSween, 'if you didn't have to go killing and injuring people.'

'But that's what the army's for, lad. And war is glorious.'

'No,' said Charley, setting his jaw, 'the *army* is glorious, with its fine red and green uniforms and its smart parades, and its bands and marching music, and the way things are tidy and neat, but war makes all that a shambles. War takes a glorious army and smashes it all to bits.

'I think the army should make a fine show just for the people to watch. I don't think it should go to war at all. We polish our boots and wax the wooden stocks on the rifles. See what happens, McSween? We shine the brass cannons and paint the limbers a nice colour. We huff on the peaks of our shakos, so they gleam in the sun. We oil our swords so they glisten. And for what, McSween? So we can march into battle and have them covered in dirt and somebody's blood.'

'Well . . .' said the veteran soldier, unsure of his ground now the argument had been put to him.

'And on top of all that,' continued Charley heatedly, 'we let men be killed, and we kill other men, just because they're standing on a bit of mud we want to stand on.'

'Well . . .'

'It doesn't make sense to me, McSween. I want no part of it any longer.'

'Ah, as to that, Bates, you 'aven't a choice, because they've got you, you see. There's no resignin' from this man's army – not unless you're an orficer – which you ain't,' he pointed out. 'And there's an end to it.'

But it wasn't an end to it as far as Charley was concerned, for he had a secret.

Some minutes later the thunder of horses' hooves was heard at the end of the valley. The Russian army had returned. The British were under attack again, but this time Prince Menshikov sent in his cavalry first. The Hussars came riding towards Balaclava, thousands of them. If they got through to the harbour, all the British ships would be in danger because the main British infantry divisions were miles away, besieging Sebastopol.

There was only a small force which stood between the mighty Russian cavalry and their goal. One solitary regiment, one single battalion of a thousand men.

162

The 93rd Sutherland Highlanders.

'McSween,' cried a corporal who only had one arm. 'Get your rifle quick. They need us at the entrance to the gorge.'

'What?' cried McSween, dropping a bundle of blankets he was carrying. 'Who needs us?'

'The Russians are coming. They're charging down the valley now. If they're not stopped we'll all be killed and Balaclava will be lost. It's been asked that all the walking wounded go to assist the 93rd. They have spread themselves in a thin red line across the mouth of the gorge and Sir Colin Campbell has ordered them to stand or die.'

'The 93rd?' cried McSween. 'Sir Colin Campbell? Is he there?'

'Leading from the front,' replied the corporal. 'Quick, get your rifle or we shall fail in our duty.'

McSween was a malingerer, a man who avoided any task if at all possible, yet now he jumped to his feet. Here was the chance of a lifetime for him. Now he could show his Scottish ancestors, those ghosts of his past, that he was ready to fight and die alongside fellow countrymen.

He had been denied the chance to join the

Highland Brigade, possibly because of his history as a troublemaker before he joined the army. The Highland regiments were more fussy than others about who they recruited into their ranks. Now they needed him and he went willingly.

'Let's go, corporal,' he said eagerly. 'Let's go, or we shall miss all the fun.'

Charley followed the group of some sixty men on the sick list who could actually stand and fire a rifle without falling over. Some of the wives were there too, standing back, for if the Russians got through there would be no safe hiding place. Better to be out in the open where they could at least try to run.

Charley saw McSween take his place in the thin red line. He heard him call to Sir Colin Campbell, a grey-moustached figure who sat astride a tall horse.

'Private McSween, here, sir. Stand or die, that's my motto. You can rely on a countryman like meself.'

'You sound like a cockney, McSween,' roared back that old warhorse from his saddle, 'but if you're willing to fight to the death then we're proud to have you in our ranks.'

'Thank you, sir,' said McSween, with a little sigh, hoping his Scottish forebears had heard the great

Colin Campbell. 'Proud to be of service.'

Charley watched with shallow breath as several thousand Russian Hussars came hurtling down the valley, the dust billowing like mist about the horsemen. Their sabres were drawn and they swished them through the air. Sunlight glinted on hilt and pommel. It scythed down the curved blades, to flash like slivers of broken mirrors. Over their shoulders were slung short carbines. The clank and clatter of their bits and bridle-rings, their sabre scabbards, was frightening to hear. It was the rattle of death, charging towards the line of red-coated, kilted soldiers, who stood waiting calmly. At the head of the Russian horde was a grey-haired general on a white horse. He waved his sword in the air, encouraging his Hussars onward.

'Steady, lads, steady,' said Sir Colin. 'Don't fire until I give the word.'

Charley could hear the thunder of the hooves, drumming a steady tattoo on the hard valley floor. The ground began to shake beneath his feet. It seemed to him that even the distant mountain peaks were trembling.

'FIRE!' came the brusque command from Sir Colin.

A volley shattered the polite morning air as a thousand rifles crashed out simultaneously. Gunsmoke wafted back to where the watchers stood, Charley among them. Already the 93rd and extras were reloading, their long ramrods clattering in the barrels.

'Steady, lads. Aim. FIRE!'

A second volley ripped out, roaring down the valley.

This time the Russian horsemen were checked in their stride. Some fell. Wounded men still in their saddles rode off to the sides of the gorge. The grey-haired general was nowhere to be seen. His white horse was running riderless back to the Russian lines, the brass stirrups dancing empty on the ends of their leather straps.

Now the Russian cavalry was very close, not more than two-hundred yards away. Again, the ramrods rattled down the barrels, the percussion caps went on, the rifles were levelled.

'FIRE!'

This time, because men had hurried their loading, and some were faster than others, the volley was more ragged, a series of shots which jumped down the line like explosions down a string of firecrackers. The

Russians took the fusillade head on. The lead horsemen veered off to the left, the rest of the brigade following them. Charley and the others watching could not believe it. The Russian cavalry had been turned!

'We've done it,' cried Sir Colin Campbell, in a voice of disbelief. '*You've* done it, lads. Hurrah for the Sutherland Highlanders. They're beaten. They've had enough. Hurrah, hurrah, hurrah.'

In the midst of this euphoria, Mrs Duberly went galloping by on Bob, determined to reach a high hill from which she could see the rest of the battle.

'Hurrah!' she cried, as she went past with her hat ribbons flying. 'Hurrah for the 93rd!' She rode out almost through the middle of the retreating Russian cavalry, towards the ridge on which Lord Raglan had gathered his staff in order to conduct the rest of the day's fighting, for there was surely more to come.

Sir Colin took off his bonnet and threw it in the air. The rest of the riflemen, McSween included, did the same. Their cheers echoed out over the whole valley. They had been prepared to stand or die, and their steadfastness had destroyed the Russian cavalry's confidence. There were not many casualties amongst the enemy, but the fact that these few riflemen had been prepared to stand rock-solid and meet a cavalry charge head on – a charge of superior numbers – had been enough to win the hour.

McSween's face was shining with pride as the Russian horsemen went thundering away into the main valley. Balaclava harbour had been saved by the 93rd Sutherland Highlanders, with a little help from Private McSween and the invalids from the hospital.

'Well done indeed, men,' said Sir Colin Campbell again. 'Look – look what's happening. The Russian cavalry have gone up into the valley and the Heavy Brigade are charging them.'

Charley dashed forward to a little knoll and stood on top of it. From there he could see the Heavy Brigade, consisting of squadrons of the Royal Dragoons, Scots Greys and the Inniskilling Dragoons on their large horses. They were led by the elderly General Scarlett. They were not so dashing as the Light Brigade, but every bit as courageous and skilful. The Greys, Royals and Inniskillings charged into the enemy with battle moans and battle yells and much bravado.

The Heavy Brigade were as outnumbered on horseback as the 93rd had been on foot, but they fought so valiantly the Russian cavalry once more gave up the fight. Charley saw the enemy squadrons wheel away in confusion as more of the Heavy Brigade came riding up in clouds of dust. The whole of the Russian cavalry was now riding back into the hills in great disarray. Cheers again went up from the big farm lads on their tall horses as they waved their swords in the air in triumph.

'Did you see that?' cried McSween, his delight unbounded. 'The Heavies did it! They routed the Ruskies. We've won the day again.'

But McSween spoke too soon. Not long after that the Light Brigade, under Lord Cardigan's command, rode into the valley of death. A misunderstood order carried by a staff officer, Captain Nolan, sent them charging into the mouths of the enemy guns, and all down the sides of the valley were Russian infantry who made them run a gauntlet of withering fire. Beyond the Russian cannons were the Russian cavalry, waiting to get their revenge.

Captain Nolan was the first man killed, but many others lost their lives. The Light Brigade was massacred. The survivors of the 17th Lancers, the 11th Hussars, the 13th Light Dragoons, and others, came limping back in tatters. The Heavy Brigade tried charging again, but they too were beaten back by enemy fire.

The day was neither won nor lost. The Battle of Balaclava forced the Russians to retreat, but the British had lost its pride and glory, its wonderful light cavalry.

Cleaning his rifle that night, with Charley sitting watching him, McSween said, 'This day will be talked about forevermore, you mark my words, boy. We've fought on the ground where history's been made, that's certain sure.'

Charley was not thinking of victory or valour at that moment though. He was remembering the sound of the dignified, slow Russian retreat, back up into the hills. In particular, he was recalling the sound of the drummers. He could not see their faces, their uniforms. It could have been him and Swinburn wielding the drumsticks.

The next day on parade, while Charley's company was standing to attention as Lieutenant Pickering with Sergeant Bilford inspected them, Charley quietly removed his shako and took off his drum. He placed them carefully on the ground.

170

Then he walked towards Mrs Duberly, who was standing with Dr Porter, watching the parade.

Sergeant Bilford almost choked.

'Oi! Where do you think you're goin', lad?'

Charley turned and lifted her chin.

'I'm leaving the army, sergeant.'

The sergeant looked as if he were about to explode.

'You're *what*? You get back here now – on the double, boy – or I'll have your guts for garters.'

'Don't call me boy – I'm a girl.'

Sergeant Bilford seemed not to hear, for he stormed forward, his face red and his beard bristling. Charley knew the sergeant had not been so humiliated in front of an officer before, but there had been no other way. Charley had reached the end of her tether. She could not stay in the army one second longer.

'You – you insubordinate soldier!' yelled Sergeant Bilford. 'Get back in them ranks *now*!'

Mrs Duberly came across and put her hand on Charley's shoulder.

'Now, Charley, let me ask you a question. What is your full name? It's not really *Charles* Bates, is it?'

Charley's head shook.

'What is it then?' asked Mrs Duberly gently.

'Charlotte, ma'am. I'm Charlotte Mary Bates. And now Danny Swinburn's been killed I don't want to fight in the war any more. I want to go home.'

'A girl?' said Sergeant Bilford in a quiet disbelieving voice, as the penny finally dropped. 'A girl drummer boy?'

McSween laughed out loud from the ranks. 'Our Charley-boy, a girl? There's a turn up. Had you there, sergeant, eh?'

Lieutenant Pickering was shaking his head sagely. Ever the practical man, he said, 'Had us all, I'm afraid. Well, there's not a lot we can do about it now. Mrs Duberly, can you make sure that what Private Bates is saying is the truth? Though I'm sure this isn't a lie. You can tell by the child's face.'

Charley slipped her hand into that of Mrs Duberly and they walked away.

The lieutenant called after them, 'We can't have drummer girls in the 44th, I'm afraid. The colonel will have apoplexy. We'll have to make arrangements to return her to England.'

Mrs Duberly waved by way of reply, then she turned to Charley and asked, 'Would you like to go home now? Perhaps your mother's missing you, Charlotte?'

'No, she's dead – like my friend Danny Swinburn.'

'It's very sad about Private Swinburn, but a lot of good men died yesterday. He was not the only one.'

'Danny wasn't a man,' Charley reminded her quietly. 'He was only a young boy.'

15 Voyage to Scutari

Charley went with Mrs Duberly to her room in a small white house overlooking the harbour, where British cargo ships jostled each other for space on the waterfront. When they emerged, Charley was wearing a dress. Mrs Duberly had made it out of material from one of her own gowns. She had also fashioned a coat from a cut-down hacking jacket.

In the meantime, the lieutenant told Colonel Peters Charley's revelation.

'Of course, we must send her home,' agreed the colonel. 'A girl drummer in the 44th? It's unthinkable. Isn't Dr Porter due to go to Scutari soon, to help out there? He shall take the girl with him.'

'I think that's a very good idea, colonel.'

The barracks at Constantinople was now being used as a hospital. A ship with the British wounded from the Battle of Balaclava was departing in the morning. There were rumours amongst the army personnel, put about by the war correspondent for *The Times*, Mr William Russell, that a lady from England was gathering nurses and would arrive at Scutari shortly.

Her name was Miss Florence Nightingale.

Charley shared the room in the little white house with Mrs Duberly. She watched the ships anchoring as supplies began coming through. At last the surgeons had enough candles to be able to work at night on those who needed their skills.

'Are you going to take me home, doctor?' Charley asked Dr Porter that evening. 'Are we going back to Rochford? For I shan't be able to find my way back there without someone to show me the way.'

'I shall be taking you as far as Scutari, Charlotte. You remember, the place where you and Swinburn caught all the rats. I'm afraid they may still need your expertise there. The rats are just as numerous. Perhaps even more so.'

'I hear they creep in and steal the food from the patients' mouths,' said Mrs Duberly. 'I hope Miss Nightingale can stop it.'

Sir John Hall was in charge of Scutari Hospital. He had done little to improve the cleanliness. He had not even supplied the patients' basic needs, like cutlery or clean clothes, or decent bedlinen. Mostly men slept on rough canvas sheets which chafed their skin, and they ate with their fingers.

'It was Swinburn who was so good at rat-catching,' said Charley sadly, 'but I will try without him.'

'There are surely better tasks for a young lady than catching vermin?' said Mrs Duberly. 'In a medical establishment there are things like fetching and carrying for the patients, and helping them with their eating.'

'Yes,' the doctor agreed. 'It might be well that you should get some practice in, Charlotte. Why not come to the little hospital at the back of the village tomorrow? I shall find something for you to do there, to get you out from under Mrs Duberly's feet, kind lady though she is.'

The following day Charley went to the cottage

hospital. They used her there to run errands and to generally fetch and carry. She enjoyed being useful. McSween was now there. He had caught some kind of fever. Perhaps McSween of all the people who knew Charley was tickled the most by the fact that she was a girl. 'It's not often people get the better of the military,' he said.

16 Florence Nightingale's assistant

The Battle of Balaclava left the whole fate of the war in the Crimea undecided. If the allies had followed up their advantage after the Battle of the Alma and pursued the retreating Russian army, it would have all been over. They could have taken Sebastopol and that would have been that. The Russians would have had to give up their ideas for a new Russian Empire and the British and French could have gone home.

As it was, every day the Russians were fortifying the city of Sebastopol, and the allies did nothing but watch.

'You and I are going to be out of it from now on,' the doctor told Charley. 'We're catching a ship tomorrow morning for Constantinople.'

'Good,' said Charley. 'I'm fed up with this place, now that Swinburn's not here. It's nothing but rain and mud. I like Mrs Duberly, but there's always lots of officers around her. You can't get to see her much.'

'That's true,' the doctor replied, smiling ruefully.

'Doctor,' said Charley seriously. 'Do you think Swinburn would have asked me to marry him – you know, once we were grown-ups?'

'Undoubtedly,' replied the assistant-surgeon. 'I'm sure he would have done. Of course, he never knew you were a girl, did he? You did not tell him, I suppose?'

'No, I didn't tell anyone,' answered Charley. 'I was afraid they'd send me back if they knew. And you can't stay friends with someone *all* the time, can you? I mean, if me and Swinburn had a fight, he might go off and tell the colonel, just to spite me. So I kept it a secret.'

'Very wise of you. I can't help wondering too, how those slave traders would have felt if they had known you were a girl. It was probably galling enough for their leader to be knocked into the water by a young boy – but a young *girl*? I think he might have died of shame.'

The following day the pair of them stood on the waterfront by the gangway, ready to board their ship. Mrs Duberly had come to see them off. So had Privates McSween and Wilson. Charley was quite famous now. One of the French *cantinières* had sent her a letter, which the doctor translated, telling her she was a heroine and an example to all women with a sense of adventure.

> *These men think they can do everything and we women can do nothing when it comes to things physical, but of course this is all rubbish. You have proved that there is no difference. A girl can do as well as a boy, a woman as well as any man. Charlotte Bates, I salute you as an Amazon princess.*
>
> *Au revoir*
>
> *Jeannette Dubois*

'Why is this French lady writing to me?' Charley had asked. 'Does she know me?'

'It's because you are so well known to everyone in the Crimea now, Charlotte. If you stayed here much longer people would come from miles around just to see your face. Prince Menshikov himself would be asking for an audience with you. The drummer girl of the Battle of the Alma!'

Charley said her goodbyes on a grey Crimean day. The skies were heavy and resting on the shoulders of the distant hills. Birds seemed to be forcing their way through the dull air by sheer tenacity alone. Dark buildings with squinting, short-sighted windows looked out over a blustery, choppy ocean.

'Well, *bon voyage*, my dear,' said Mrs Duberly. 'I'm sorry you are going, for there are sure to be many more exciting battles to come and you will miss them all.'

Charlotte, dressed in her cut-down clothes, dropped a dainty curtsy, as neatly as any debutante at her presentation to the queen.

'Thank you, ma'am, but I'm pleased to be going.'

McSween, his eyes quite misty with the occasion, bent down and offered a grizzled cheek.

'Will you give us a goodbye kiss, Charlotte?'

181

'No, I will not,' said a horrified Charley. 'Your face is dirty as usual, McSween.'

He straightened and grinned, not at all put out.

'That's certain. So is Wilson's. We don't believe in water, do we, Wilson?'

'Bad for you,' confirmed Wilson, 'inside or out.'

The two rough men shook hands with Charley and told her she had been the best drummer the regiment had ever known.

'You do tell lies, McSween, and you, Wilson – but I've always liked you both.'

The pair of reprobates grinned.

A brass bell sounded on the quarterdeck of the ship.

'Well, Charlotte, we must be going,' said the doctor. 'You can wave to your friends from the deck.'

So they went up the gangway. A little while later the ship set sail, bound for Constantinople over the Black Sea. This time Charlotte would have no duties on board. Nor would she have her Swinburn to lead her in and out of mischief. The doctor spent the time on board attempting to teach her to read the Bible. She liked the stories – David and Goliath, Moses, Jesus performing his miracles – but Charley did not get very far with her learning. She was too anxious about what was going to happen to her. Now she was not at all sure she wanted to go back to England, but would there be enough for her to do at Scutari Hospital?

The day Charley and the doctor entered Scutari Hospital again was one of weak sunshine, heralding the coming winter.

Since the doctor's services were needed immediately, he had no time to make sure Charley was settled in properly. However, she remembered Scutari from the time she had been there with the regiment and she found herself a place to sleep in one of the corners of the corridors. She was near enough to answer an urgent summons from the wards, but far away enough to sleep properly.

She did not want to stay in one of the wards, the huge billets, where the patients were laid out in long lines. Men died in there every night.

The floors were still infested with lice and cockroaches, and the rats stole from the plates of weak patients even as they ate their food. The cries of those in pain were pitiful. There were only a few doctors, struggling against a storm of problems, unable to cope with the numbers.

Charley did her best for the men. She could not read to them, but she told them news of the outside world when she heard it. She brought them water and food and generally made herself useful.

One day Charley was washing the face of a soldier when she felt the light touch of a hand on her shoulder. She turned and looked up to see a woman wearing a lace bonnet over hair parted neatly in the middle. The lady was not particularly pretty, but her features were even and pleasant. It was her eyes which held Charley in thrall for a moment though. They were kindly eyes, but strong, with a determined look to them. Charley knew this woman would stand no nonsense from anyone, child or adult.

'And who have we here? Are you the daughter of one of the regiment wives?'

'No, ma'am,' answered Charley, awed by the presence of this grand personage. For some reason Charley found it necessary to trot out her full name. 'I'm Charlotte Mary Bates.'

A puzzled little frown came to the forehead of the young woman, then her face assumed an expression of enlightenment.

'Of course. Dr Porter has spoken of you. You're

184

Charley, the drummer girl, aren't you?' The woman smiled and put out a slim hand. 'I'm pleased to meet you, Miss Charlotte Mary Bates. My name is Miss Florence Nightingale.'

'Oh! You're the lady who's bringing the nurses to help.'

'Indeed that's who I am. And I should be very happy for your continued assistance, Charlotte, if you're willing to give it?'

'Oh, yes, ma'am, for I've nowhere else to go really.'

'What about your home? Do you have parents?'

'Only my dad. He's never there. I sleep with Sam, the big dray horse, ma'am.'

'Ah, you sleep in a stable.'

'Yes, ma'am – just like the Baby Jesus,' Charlotte said, grinning.

At that moment one of Miss Nightingale's nurses came hurrying up to her.

'Miss Florence, I've been to the laundry. There hasn't been a bedsheet washed for months. There are hundreds of men lying sick here and I'm told only *eleven* nightshirts have been laundered since the hospital opened . . .'

'Then we must obtain some soap and set to work,' replied Miss Nightingale briskly. 'What about blankets? Most of the patients seem to have canvas sailcloth for bedclothes.'

'There are plenty of shirts and blankets, not to say soap and other stores, but they are still in packages down at the warehouse on the quay. The man in charge of the stores will not let us open them, for he says he has not received the certificate which allows us to undo the bundles and crates.'

Miss Nightingale stiffened, her lips forming a thin line.

'Did he say when this certificate might arrive?'

'In four months or so, when the certificate has been passed by the several departments who have to sign it in England.'

'Charlotte,' said Miss Nightingale firmly, 'come and see justice being done.'

With that, Florence Nightingale marched off, followed by Charley and a number of her nurses. She went down to the quay and without even speaking to the protesting storeman, began opening all the bundles and crates.

'I shall get into terrible trouble,' wailed the

storeman. 'I shall be admonished.'

Miss Nightingale took absolutely no notice of his tantrum. She had been in the hospital only two days and she was already appalled by the suffering caused by silly rules and regulations. She was having none of it. She was a powerful woman with the backing of Queen Victoria herself, and she was going to see the hospital run efficiently. If it meant clashing with the army, then she was prepared to clash.

Within a week all the men's shirts had been washed, they had clean blankets on their beds, and the problem of lice and cockroaches was being tackled. Florence Nightingale's mission was to see that chaos was turned into order. This she did in no uncertain manner, writing hard truths in letters to people in England when it became necessary, and having terrible rows with Sir John Hall, the head of the hospital, whom she regarded as a tyrant and an incompetent man.

'The patients need soap as much as they need your surgeon's knife,' she told him. 'They need comfort and proper food. They need clean conditions. They need cutlery to eat with. Do you eat with your fingers? No, of course not! Then why should they?'

'You are spoiling them,' he cried vehemently. 'We do not need your prissy female ways here!'

'Oh, but you do, sir,' she retorted, 'and you've got them, whether you like it or not.'

Sir John Hall tried to starve out Florence Nightingale but she had brought her own food to Scutari.

It was a hopeless task trying to get rid of her. She transformed the hospital into a clean and efficient medical establishment, despite Sir John Hall's efforts to stop her. As for Charley, she would have followed Miss Nightingale into fire and flood.

Dr Porter was posted back to the Crimea some time after Miss Nightingale arrived. The army have a habit of sending people hither and thither without any real overall plan. He said goodbye to Charley and promised he would keep track of her movements through Miss Nightingale.

'Goodbye, Dr Porter,' said Charley, giving him a warm smile with her handshake. She had become quite the little lady since one of the nurses, Julia Swanlock, had taken her in hand. She wore well-made, sensible dresses and caps, and she was being given schooling. Her command of English had improved considerably. 'Please convey my regards to Wilson and McSween.'

The doctor assumed a grave expression. 'Ah, as to them, I'm afraid I have to tell you that Private Wilson was killed while carrying out picquet duty on the siege line at Sebastopol.'

'Oh,' said Charley, looking down. 'I'm sorry for that, Dr Porter.'

'Yes, so am I,' he replied sombrely. 'However, you may be heartened to hear that your friend Private McSween distinguished himself at the Battle of Inkerman and has been promoted to a lance-corporal. That's good news, isn't it?'

Charley shook her head and pursed her lips. 'Poor McSween, now he'll have to behave himself, won't he, Dr Porter. He'll hate doing that, you know. I expect he'll soon be a private again, when he gets himself into trouble.'

The doctor laughed, thinking her insight had not suffered during her time at Scutari.

'I'm sure you are right, Charley. McSween is not one of those men who takes easily to the straight and narrow. But you never know, he may end up a field-marshal and surprise us all. Some human beings have a tendency to do that.'

'Not McSween,' said Charley, shaking her head sagely. 'Even Lance-Corporal McSween does not really sound right, does it? Think of *Field-Marshal* McSween.'

They both laughed.

The doctor made ready to board ship, but Charley suddenly took his hand and held it for a moment. She looked up into his eyes.

'Dr Porter, will you put some flowers on Swinburn's grave, please? And please tell him I sent them. Say I miss him because . . . because . . . because he is a *rascal.*'

'I shall do as you say. Goodbye, Charlotte.'

'Goodbye, Dr Porter.'

*

Dr Porter never saw Charley again, but he heard good reports of her. She did not return home after the Crimean War ended, but went on to India with some other nurses. Ten years after the end of the Crimean war the doctor learned that a certain Miss Charlotte Mary Bates had helped to transform a hospital in Calcutta from a place of poor hygiene and negligence to one of good standing and efficiency.

Author's note

In order to satisfy any curiosity on the subject, it is a fact that not only were there children on the battlefields of terrible nineteenth century conflicts, but there were indeed women fighting alongside the men. They were, of course, disguised as men for various reasons.

Six wives per 100 men were allowed in the Crimean War. This meant that if a wife wanted to be with her husband, and she was not chosen, she had to cut her hair short and join the regiment in the guise of a man.

Others joined as men because soldiers were paid. A woman in dire straits in the nineteenth century was thrown on the mercy of the parish authorities. If she did not want to go to the poorhouse, the workhouse or receive meagre charity, she might consider a job in the army as a way out of her problems. These 'military maids' were often only discovered when their bodies were stripped for the funeral after they had been found dead on the battlefield.

One of the British army's chief medical officers at the Crimea, Dr James Barry, was in fact Miranda Barry, who had disguised herself as a man in order to be able to take medical training and become a doctor – a profession forbidden to women in those times.

Other recorded famous military maids were:

Deborah Sampson, who took part in the American Revolution as Robert Shurtleff.

Loreta Janeta Velasquez, who fought in the American Civil War as Harry T. Buford.

Hannah Snell, an English soldier and sailor of the late eighteenth century, who called herself James Gray.

Flora Sandes, who became a sergeant in the French army.

Angelique Bruton, who fought with Napoleon's army.

Valerie Arkell-Smith, who rose to the rank of colonel under the name of Barker.

There were women in uniform then, women who fought as men, just as there are women in uniform today.

There are also children, still as young as ten years old, on the battlefields of modern wars today, bearing arms and dying for causes few of them understand.

Names of real people

Lord Cardigan, commander of the Light Brigade of cavalry at Balaclava.

Mrs Duberly, wife of Paymaster Henry Duberly and her horse, Bob.

Lord Raglan, commander-in-chief of the Army of the East.

Lieutenant-General Sir George Brown, commander of the Light Division.

Major-General Sir Richard England, commander of the Third Division.

Charles Darwin, English naturalist.

Duke of Wellington, commander-in-chief of the British army at the Battle of Waterloo, 1815 – thirty-eight years before the Crimean War.

Mary Seacole, West Indian lady who nursed the troops at the Crimean War.

Dr James Barry, medical officer at the Crimean War.

Marshal St Arnaud, commander-in-chief of the French army.

Prince Menshikov, commander-in-chief of the Russian army.

Dasha Aleksandrovna, eleven-year-old Russian orphan, a heroine who sold the few things she owned to buy a pony, cart and medical supplies, so that she could brave the battlefields of the Crimea in order to comfort abandoned soldiers.

William Russell, war correspondent for *The Times* newspaper.

Florence Nightingale.

Sir John Hall, surgeon in charge of Scutari Hospital.

Sir Colin Campbell, commander of the Highland Brigade and hero of Balaclava.

Brigadier-General Scarlett, commander of the Heavy Brigade of cavalry at Balaclava.

Captain Nolan, staff officer.

Garry Kilworth

The Drowners

'Always treat a river with respect,' John Timbrell told each of
his many children, when they reached an age of understanding.
*'Never take her for granted. She don't strike often, but when
she do, it's quick as an adder. River's got no concerns for age
nor whether you be a boy or a girl. It'll take what's there, and
never a thank'ee left behind.'*

Tom Timbrell heeds his father's warning but still the river takes
him – and with him goes the knowledge of the drowning of the
fields, which the local farmers rely upon for the successful
tending of their land.

For two years the farmers struggle hopelessly until, one day,
a mysterious young boy appears and begins to teach Jem
Blunden the ways of the river, a boy whose age remains
untouched by the passing of the years and who bears a
remarkable resemblance to Tom Timbrell . . .

'A fine, exciting story, beautifully told.'
Leon Garfield

Shortlisted for the Carnegie Medal

Garry Kilworth

The Phantom Piper

'I thought it was a dream, but there was a piper. He was playing a pibroch. He stood up on a high crag till all the grown-ups reached him, then he went off. They went with him. Followed him like sheep. Followed the music he was making.'

The Children of Canlish Glen are abandoned. They know there is only way to get their parents and families back, but if they do not succeed by Hogmanay, history may repeat itself and all the adults will die.

Then the strangers arrive. They come out of nowhere – as the parents went into nowhere – and they are dangerous . . .

'Pulsating stuff . . .'
Michael Morpurgo, *Guardian*

'Strong dramatic fantasy . . . This is not just a tense and frightening suspense story; it is also a kind of *Lord of the Flies* in reverse . . .'
Junior Bookshelf

Garry Kilworth

The Brontë Girls

'Papa doesn't like us mixing with the outside world. He says the twentieth century is a monstrous place.'

When Chris trespasses on the isolated Craster farm, Emily Craster is fascinated by him. She is almost fifteen and has known no other life except that with her two sisters and parents on the farm – modelled on the Brontës' parsonage at Haworth. Emily is determined to get to know Chris – but her actions will smash her family's world apart . . .

'Garry Kilworth has seized upon a brilliant idea and developed it with his neat inventiveness into a fascinating tale of family conflict and youthful love.'
Junior Bookshelf

Shortlisted for the Carnegie Medal